THE SHEIKH'S SECRET SON

BY

MAGGIE COX

MILLS
BOON

First published in Great Britain 2017
By Mills & Boon, an imprint of HarperCollins*Publishers*
1 London Bridge Street, London, SE1 9GF

Large Print edition 2017

© 2017 Maggie Cox

ISBN: 978-0-263-07103-0

Printed and bound in Great Britain
by CPI Antony Rowe, Chippenham, Wiltshire

To Alicia Barber
A unique young woman
who has become a very dear friend x

CHAPTER ONE

THE FALL FROM the granite wall happened in an instant, yet strangely time seemed to slow down as Darcy saw herself plunge downwards. It was like an uncanny out-of-body experience. Her mind flashed—happening but *not* happening—just like in a dream. Trouble was, she'd lost concentration due to her mind being dominated by the nerve-racking task at hand—which was hopefully to see the charismatic owner of the regal manor and to tell him at last that their passionate affair had produced a son...

Now, the searing knife-like pain that shot through her ankle as she hit the ground gave her something even more pertinent to worry about. Issuing a string of unladylike curses, she rubbed at the offending bone, wincing as the pain intensified excruciatingly. *How on earth was she going to stand?* The flesh was already reddening and swelling—too fast for her liking. No chance of presenting the poised unruffled appearance she'd had in mind, then...

Even as the realisation descended a heavy-set man in a slightly snug black suit started running towards her from the other side of the splendid gardens. It didn't take much guessing to deduce that he was a security guard. She reminded herself of her intention to stay as calm as possible, no matter what occurred. Then she made herself breathe deeply to try to control the waves of pain that washed over her.

When the man got to her, his breath hitting the frigid October air in tangible puffs of steam, she saw that his fleshy olive complexion was coated with a fine sheen of perspiration.

Despite her dilemma, Darcy quipped, 'You could have saved yourself the effort. I'm clearly not going anywhere any time soon. I think I've twisted my ankle.'

'You are a very silly young woman to risk such a foolish thing. I can tell you now that the Sheikh is not going to be very happy.'

Her realisation that he was referring to the man she'd desperately hoped to see made her feel as though she'd slammed *into* the wall rather than merely falling off it.

'His Highness is the owner of this property and you are trespassing. I have to warn you that he will not take the intrusion lightly.'

'No...I don't suppose he will.'

However her ex-lover reacted when he saw her, it surely couldn't make her feel any worse than she felt already. *Yes, it could.* Darcy had been on edge *before* the accident, never mind now, with the looming possibility of being confronted by him and accused of breaking and entering.

'Look, what's happened has happened, and as much as I need to explain my motives for being here to His Highness, first I'm going to need your help in getting to my feet.'

'That is not a good idea. You need to be checked

over by a doctor first. Trying to stand might make the injury worse.'

Staring up at the guard, she witnessed an unexpected glimpse of concern in his chocolate-brown eyes. Then he withdrew a phone from his jacket and spoke to someone at the other end in a language that she was only too familiar with from her days of working at the bank. To make matters worse, the recognition brought with it a vividly searing memory that she expressly didn't welcome right then—especially when she'd stupidly put herself in the mother of all awkward situations.

And all because she'd been driven to scale a wall she never should have attempted in the first place, resulting in a highly inconvenient injury.

But what else was she supposed to do when the necessity of seeing her former lover was becoming ever more urgent? Her worst fears had come true. *He was engaged to be married.* No matter how many times she reminded herself of the fact, her heart vehemently rejected the idea as though it was poison.

At the same time Darcy realised the guard really *wasn't* going to help her to her feet, he abruptly ended his call. Then he withdrew a voluminous handkerchief from his pocket and proceeded to mop his brow.

'The doctor is coming. I have also arranged for you to have some water.'

'I don't need water. I just need some help to get to my feet.'

Suddenly aware that any further attempts to ask for his assistance were futile, Darcy let her head drop with a grimace and the silken wheat-coloured hair that had escaped from her loosely arranged topknot glided down over her cheekbones. She could only pray it was helping to disguise the shock and fear that were pulsating through her. Surrendering to weakness for even the shortest time was anathema to her. The last time she had done such a thing it had cost her dear.

'Who is this doctor, anyway, and will he call an ambulance?'

'You do not need an ambulance. The doctor who is coming is the Sheikh's very own physician. He is highly qualified and has an apartment here.'

'Then I don't suppose I have much choice but to wait for him. I hope he's got some strong painkillers.'

'If you need to take painkillers then you also need water. Do you want me to call someone to inform them that you have had an accident?'

Darcy's heartbeat rapidly quickened. Her mother would hardly take the news calmly. Not when she was apt to turn the slightest mishap into a drama worthy of a soap opera. The last thing she wanted was for her parent's anxiety to spill over to her little boy and worry him.

'No. I don't… Thanks all the same.' Her smile at the guard was tentatively hopeful, but she suspected he didn't believe a word she said.

Because of the dwindling daylight, she hadn't

noticed the two figures hurriedly heading to-wards them from the manor house. But she noticed them *now*. There was definitely the suggestion of urgency in their quickened steps as they started to run.

Deliberately glancing away, Darcy winced as she rubbed at her swollen ankle.

Would the next people to arrive on the scene be the police, to charge her with breaking and entering?

As if intuiting her distress, her companion dropped down in front of her and consolingly patted her arm. Her blue eyes widened in surprise. His behaviour was hardly typical of any security official she knew of. But just then, when she was feeling alone and frightened, despite her fake bravado, the man's kindness was appreciated.

'The doctor will soon tend to your ankle. Do not distress yourself unduly.'

'I'm not distressed. I'm just angry that I climbed the wall. I meant no harm by it. I just wanted to take a peek at the house in the hope that…in the hope that if I saw the Sheikh I might speak with him.'

Her teeth clamped down on her lip as the man's perusal suddenly grew more interested, and she found herself hostage to an uncharacteristic wave of self-pity.

With her voice quavering, she said, 'I read in the newspaper that he had moved here. I used to work for him, you know?'

'Then if you wanted to see him again, you should have rung his office and made an appointment.'

'I've tried doing that, many times, but I was told by his secretary that he had to agree to it first. She never got back to me, no matter how many times I tried. In truth, I don't think he even got my messages.'

'I am sure he did. Perhaps His Highness has his reasons for not contacting you?'

'Rashid.'

The deep bass voice behind them had them

both immediately turning their heads. The impressive Arabian attire of the owner of the voice added to Darcy's profound sense of shock when her gaze fell upon his features. His sublimely carved face was etched deep into her memory, but the last time she'd seen it their time together had culminated in a deed that had devastatingly broken her heart. Yet, despite that, her instinct was to greet him with familiarity.

Zafir...

Thankfully she checked the impulse just in time. His haunting black eyes were staring at her hard, she saw, piercing her like the glowing points of a dagger. Although she shuddered, she still drank him in, realising that although he looked a little older he was still as handsome as sin and must still set women's hearts fluttering from here to Kathmandu.

He had also grown his hair.

It fell way past his magnificent shoulders in glossy black waves. The disturbing recollection that the dark strands were like the finest silk to touch made her guiltily yearn to experience running her fingers through the new length…

'The young lady fell off the wall, Your Highness,' the guard interjected, sounding inexplicably protective, 'and she is hurt.'

'Hurting is what she is good at.'

Stung by the bitterly voiced statement, Darcy opened her mouth to protest. *He* was the one who was good at hurting…not her. Or had he so quickly erased *that* little fact from his memory?

'What are you doing here, and why are you trespassing on my property?'

'I'll tell you why—because you wouldn't take my calls or return my messages. You wouldn't even let me make an appointment to see you. God knows how many times I've tried. This was a last resort. In all honesty I would have preferred to have left you alone…but I *had* to see you.'

His glance suspicious, the autocratic man in front of her responded grimly, 'I have never, to my knowledge, received any such messages.'

Darcy's mouth turned sickeningly dry. 'You're

joking? Why wouldn't you have received them? I always told your secretary that it was urgent and confidential. Why didn't she believe me?'

'Never mind that right now... If what you say is true then I will be making my investigations. More to the point, what is the reason you want to see me, Darcy? Did you not believe me when I said I never wanted to set eyes on you again? You could hardly have expected any good to come out of our meeting.'

He leaned down to her, and even as she breathed in the exotic scent of agar that highlighted his cologne she saw the expression on his carved face was disturbingly accusing.

'How long have you known that I was here?'

Her eyes widened nervously. 'I only recently found out. There was an article in the newspaper.'

'And you saw the opportunity to get back at me for what happened in the past?'

Her blood ran cold for a moment. 'No! That wasn't the reason I wanted to find you, Zafir. Did you imagine my aim was to try and blackmail you in some way? If you think that then you couldn't be more wrong.' Tears stung the backs of her eyelids like hot springs. Swallowing hard, she continued, 'The article said that you are engaged to be married.'

'And no doubt you want to congratulate me?'

'Don't make light of my pain like that.'

As was her habit, when she was fuming at some injustice or another, she indignantly folded her arms. The movement was a little sharp, and it somehow ricocheted down to her injured ankle. She wasn't able to suppress the groan of pain that rose up inside her.

His ebony eyes darkening in concern, Zafir turned to his immaculately suited companion. 'Dr Eden. Please give the young lady some water and take a look at her ankle...*now*. It might be broken.'

Appalled that that might be the case, with a tremulous sweep of her hand Darcy pushed back her hair and stared. 'I'm sure you'd relish that, wouldn't you?' She all but grabbed at the silver flask that was proffered and imbibed a deep gulp of icy liquid before she said anything else.

As he rose to his full height, the Sheikh's expression was clearly perturbed. 'While you deserve to be punished for what you did to me, I do not take any pleasure in the fact that you have been injured. And just one more thing'

As the slim, middle-aged doctor lithely dropped down to his haunches to examine her foot, the Arabian's black eyes glinted a warning.

'Do not call me Zafir. The use of that name is permitted only to a select circle of family and friends and clearly, Miss Carrick, you should speak in deference to the hierarchy of my position...*you* are my subordinate.'

It jolted her that he'd used her surname, and it gave her little satisfaction that he'd so strongly emphasised the 'subordinate' part. The suggestion of fury in his voice made her heart contract even more. She hadn't immediately succumbed to tears at this latest encounter with him but Darcy felt like crying now.

Once upon a time she'd loved this man more than life itself. Now he sounded as though he hated her. *And all because he'd believed his brother's vindictive lies...*

'Although I can't say for certain until it's X-rayed, I think what we have here is a severe sprain, Miss Carrick.'

The doctor's slim, cool fingers were gently checking her bones for breakage and prodding the puffy skin around her ankle to inspect it. Straight away his calm assertion along with his professional expertise reinstated her hope that things weren't as disastrous as she'd feared.

A relieved sigh escaped her but then she quickly frowned. *Just who did she think she was kidding?* Things were about as disastrous as they could get. And, having intuited the mood he was in, she suspected that Zafir didn't intend to let her get off lightly for shinning up his garden wall in order to force a meeting. He was the eldest son of the ruling family in the kingdom of Zachariah, and consequently not just important but powerful too, and she knew that if her motivation hadn't been solely to tell him that he had a son and heir she would never have attempted to see him at all.

How many times did a person's self-esteem have to be stamped into the ground before they were forced to admit defeat and walk away?

'We should take you into the house so that we can make some arrangements for your care,' Dr Eden added, his grey eyes flicking towards his impressive employer for confirmation.

The first man to help her reacted first, quickly assuming what must be his esteemed position as the Sheikh's chief security guard. 'I will go and get a stretcher, Your Highness.'

'That won't be necessary, Rashid,' Zafir flashed, his icy gaze irritably scanning Darcy as she sat hunched on the new-mown lawn, massaging her ankle. 'I will carry Miss Carrick over to the house myself.'

Her immediate declaration of indignation at being treated like some extraneous piece of baggage died on her lips. In her more forgiving moments, when she'd flirted with the unlikely idea of somehow meeting up with Zafir again and having a frank conversation with him about what had *really* happened back then, it hadn't been like this. No, *never* like this… The warm, funny, erudite man she'd once worked for and fallen in love with was a very different person from the cold, embittered stranger she was faced with now.

Biting her lip, she murmured, 'I think I'd rather crawl.'

She didn't know if he'd heard her, but to add insult to injury he easily dropped down to lift her into his arms.

'I hope you don't have an accomplice in this little escapade of yours? If you do, no doubt he is long gone. Perhaps he found out that you were not so bewitching after all, and sensibly took the opportunity to flee when he had the chance?'

Swallowing down her hurt that he so naturally assumed she'd been with another man and up to no good, Darcy schooled herself to stay silent instead of reacting. But her senses were awash with pain, and a regret that thundered like a raging river in her blood.

Could he not see beyond his own prejudiced beliefs and realise the truth? Clearly not...

Without further preamble, he swept her up and marched towards the house, with the effete doctor in front and Rashid following behind—no doubt his gaze diligently sweeping the area in case anything else untoward threatened. She didn't dwell on that for long, because now her senses had to contend with the unexpected intimacy of being pressed firmly against the Arabian's chest, knowing that he took no pleasure in the sensation and that all he must feel for her was contempt.

Zafir's heart was beating double time as he carried Darcy over to the sumptuous couch in the drawing room. In his wildest dreams he'd never thought to have the opportunity to hold her again like this. When he'd banished her from his sight over four years ago he'd sworn he wouldn't even *think* of her. But something had told him even then that he was lying. The beautiful face that he'd always likened to his vision of an angel was etched on his heart, whether he wanted it to be or not.

As he helped lower her gently onto the sofa's plumped-up cushions it was no easy task, when her bewitching perfume kept infiltrating his senses and he noted that her extraordinary blue eyes still had the ability to dazzle him more than ever.

But he would be a fool if he forgot for even an instant that this woman had cruelly betrayed him. If their relationship had progressed he would have given her everything—not least his undying love and devotion—but she had thoughtlessly ruined it all by fooling around behind his back and making a play for his own brother.

Her behaviour was beyond belief. Pretending devotion was clearly just a game to her. With her angelic face and no doubt practised feminine wiles, likely she could twist any man who took her fancy round her little finger and have her way.

His brother Xavier had warned him more than once what she was capable of—although Zafir knew his notoriously charming sibling was apt to bend the truth from time to time.

But blood was thicker than water, he told himself and how could he not believe what he'd seen with his very own eyes?

In the aftermath of that shocking incident Xavier had wasted no time in giving him further details of what Darcy was *really* like, saying he'd seen the way she operated at the bank the family owned long before Zafir had appeared to run the head office in London.

The cruel scene he'd witnessed had brought an end to all his hopes. He'd found Darcy in a heated embrace with Xavier.

Her features had radiated her shock and dismay when he'd suddenly surprised them by coming into the room, and immediately she'd denied any wrongdoing. Instead she'd insisted that she'd been trying to get *away* from Xavier, *not* willingly embracing him! That in truth

Zafir's brother had been harassing her—had been doing so for months. It was *he* who should be penalised, not *her*…

'Tell the housekeeper to get a drink for my unexpected visitor.' After addressing Rashid, Zafir turned back immediately, to keep Darcy in his sight—although under the circumstances it would take nothing less than a miracle for her to be able to run away. 'What is your preference, Miss Carrick? Tea or coffee?'

The glance he gave her was neither friendly nor particularly polite. He wasn't going to grant the woman any dispensation—that was for sure. Aside from her previous misdemeanours, she had now made an unbelievable attempt to break into his house.

'Neither.'

It was hard not to be moved by the look of anxiety he saw reflected in the blonde's vivid blue eyes and, strangely, it bothered Zafir more than it should have. Was she honestly not concerned that he might call the police and prosecute her for trespass? There was no reason why he *shouldn't*, he told himself. No matter what had gone on between them in the past, he certainly didn't owe her any allegiance.

'I—I just want to know what you intend to do about all this,' she said nervously.

'Forgive me for interrupting, Your Highness,' Dr Eden interjected firmly as he came and stood by the sofa where Darcy was lying. 'But, whatever you decide to do, I'd advise that we get Miss Carrick to the hospital first, so that her injury can be X-rayed.'

Coming out of the stupor he'd fallen into while gazing at Darcy, Zafir nodded abruptly. Retrieving his mobile phone from the inside pocket of the Arabian *khandoura* he wore, he accessed the number of one of London's most exclusive private hospitals to which he had a direct line. Glancing back at his visitor as he requested an ambulance, he had a sudden notion that she might be going into shock. She was definitely looking a little flushed, and her eyelids had fluttered closed as though she barely had the strength to keep them open.

'Dr Eden.' He authoritatively addressed the medic. 'I must ask you to take Miss Carrick's temperature. It is my opinion that she looks more than a little unwell.'

'Do not be too concerned, Your Highness,' the doctor reassured him. 'It is quite a natural reaction for a person to feel faint after an accident, but I will gladly do as you ask.'

'Good.'

A short time later, satisfied with the doctor's assurance that Darcy's rise in temperature was not significant enough to be worried about, Zafir waited impatiently for the ambulance to arrive. In turn, their patient had become particularly quiet. She was clearly lost in a mysterious landscape of her own.

He had no idea what she might be thinking. Once upon a time he wouldn't have had to speculate. He had been as intimately attuned to her thoughts and feelings as any man in love could be, and he still carried the grief of her betrayal like a suppurating wound that would never heal.

The sound of an ambulance siren pierced the room's growing preternatural stillness, and it had the same impact as a lightning bolt flashing outside.

As Zafir hurried across the oak floor, with Rashid behind him, he called out over his shoulder to the doctor. 'Keep a watch on Miss Carrick. Don't let her out of your sight!'

'What do you think I'm going to do? Perform some kind of magic trick and make myself disappear? *I wish*,' Darcy grumbled sarcastically.

Zafir didn't waste time with a response. He was already at the door, throwing it wide in order to hurry out into the hallway. Addressing the man at the front door, who introduced himself as the chief paramedic, he guided him and the two other crew members into the drawing room. Darcy was resting her back against the curve of the elegant couch, as though it had taken the strain off of the accident, but in spite of her little outburst just now she wasn't able to hide the fact that she was worried.

So was Zafir. Right then, he honestly didn't know what he was going to do about the conse- quences of her fall from his garden wall *or* her startling reappearance into his life. In truth, he was still knocked sideways at seeing her again. And as yet he hadn't decided whether to pros- ecute her or not. Most people in his privileged circle wouldn't hesitate to throw the book at her.

Hadn't he learned that she wasn't to be trusted? people would say. That she was nothing but a sly opportunist…a *Jezebel.*

He could almost hear the condemning words echo round his brain. Wasting no more time in deliberating—that would have to wait until they had the X-ray results—he instructed the para- medics to do what they had to do and transport her into the ambulance.

She was wearing jeans, a deep blue woollen sweater and a short mustard-coloured jacket. And as the paramedics expertly lifted her slen- der frame onto a stretcher Zafir observed that she'd grown a little thinner since he'd seen her last. *Had she been eating properly?*

He remembered that she'd often lose her appetite when she was stressed, and even though he knew he shouldn't give a jot if something was troubling her, knew that Darcy was *nothing* to him any more, he gruffly declared, 'I will accompany my guest to the hospital.'

'Of course, Your Highness,' the paramedic responded. 'Just to reassure you, I think it's going to be a very straightforward procedure. The young lady will soon be as right as rain again—you'll see.'

He was a slightly overweight, cheerful-looking man of forty-plus, with a receding hairline—one of those dependable sorts that the great British public would probably describe as 'the salt of the earth'. And, oddly, Zafir was reassured—at least for a minute or two.

When the attentive medical staff at the hospital stretchered Darcy into an examination room, Zafir came with her. Before they'd entered Dr

Eden had given them his own efficient assessment and, in deference to his colleagues, told his employer that he would wait for him outside.

All of these events hardly reassured Darcy. The familiar scent associated with anything medical, along with the forbidding-looking examination couch, made her feel queasy, and Zafir's daunting aristocratic presence even more so. But the most pressing thing of all on her mind was her son. At present Sami was in the care of her mother, because she was babysitting him, but what if she had to tell her that she needed to stay in hospital for the night?

Darcy had never told her mother who Sami's father was, and she contemplated how she would couch her words in order to cause the least anxiety. She knew her mother would think she'd lost her mind—climbing the walls of the Sheikh's home in an attempt to speak to him. Especially when she'd ended up spraining her ankle.

Was it worth it? She could hear her mother ask. *You should have gone down the proper route of arranging a meeting with him, no matter how long it took. Look at what you've risked!*

Darcy's heart suddenly felt as heavy as a boulder inside her chest.

And that would be *before* she conveyed to her mother the fact that her ex-employer had been furious at her finding him even *before* she'd told him that he'd left her pregnant and that he now had a son.

Seeing as he was now engaged to be married, the news would hardly be the best he could receive. But, at the same time, what would the repercussions be for *her*? What if he immediately demanded custody of Sami? Or…worse still… wanted to take him back to Zachariah, away from her and all he had known for the past four years? That didn't bear thinking about.

CHAPTER TWO

DARCY HAD A splint and a crepe bandage fitted round her injured ankle. Thankfully, the X-ray had revealed no broken bones, but Darcy had badly torn the ligaments and would need at least three weeks' complete rest to help them start to heal—beginning with one full night at the hospital so that the medical staff could keep an eye on her.

That was the part that alarmed her the most. The swish, luxurious medical facility was clearly private, and there was no way on earth she could afford to spend any of her hard-earned cash on a stay here. It was essential she get home.

Zafir had gone to consult with the doctor and her need to talk to him was growing ever more urgent. The tension she was feeling was near unbearable. But just then he returned, and his arresting presence stirred the air. There was no sign of Rashid or Dr Eden.

The impact Zafir made in his impressive garb hit her anew. With his chiselled, strong-boned features and flowing dark hair his commanding appearance was enough to render anyone speechless. He was simply *magnificent*.

Propped up by a couple of plump pillows in the hospital bed, with her ankle elevated, Darcy felt her heart bump nervously against her ribs. She couldn't help feeling a little intimidated. Instinct told her that with all the drama of her fall perhaps now *wasn't* the right time to tell him about Sami, even though it was the sole reason she'd gone to his house.

Perhaps her confession should take place under more conducive circumstances? If she could arrange such a scenario, might he view her sudden unsettling appearance in his life more favourably?

Impulsively, she reached for his hand. Having

not told her mother that she'd be back late, she felt her fears about spending the night away from her young son escalating.

'I can't possibly stay the night here, Zafir. I need to get home. There—there's something important I have to do.'

Mesmerised, he stared down at the slender hand clasping his as if he couldn't quite believe it was hers. Then he lifted his head, and where previously his dark eyes had been entranced, they were now hard with suspicion. Obviously he wasn't going to be extending an olive branch to her any time soon.

'What do you have to do that's so important?' he demanded. 'Is it that you want to tell your accomplice you were unsuccessful in breaking into my house? Is that what you need to do, Darcy? Will there be repercussions for you if you don't get home tonight?'

Wrenching back her hand, she flushed indignantly. 'For goodness' sake—once and for all, I *wasn't* trying to break in and I *don't* have an accomplice. Do you think I've become so desperate and vengeful since you fired me that I'd resort to breaking in to your house when I learnt you were there?'

'I cannot attest to knowing *what* you'd resort to, Darcy. Once upon a time I thought I knew who you were,' he said soberly, 'but clearly I didn't. As for your reasons for turning up at my residence in such a dramatic way—I am his Royal Highness Sheikh Zafir el-Kalil of Zachariah, and naturally my wealth and position draws attention… not all of it innocent.'

Distraught that he clearly still thought she was a liar, when all she'd ever done was stay loyal to him and give him her devotion, she found his words hard to bear. But suddenly part of his statement registered more emphatically.

'I've just realised… That was your father's title, wasn't it? I mean…*he* was the Sheikh of Zachariah, wasn't he? Are you saying that he's passed away and now you're the…?'

'Sheikh of the kingdom… Yes, I am.'

It was as though a shutter had slammed down over his enigmatic gaze and rendered his feelings impossible to read. Was he still grieving? *He must be.* Darcy knew that father and son had been close.

As she twisted her hands together she felt genuine sympathy, unsullied by the turbulent waters that flowed between them. She knew only too well what it meant to lose a devoted father. And once upon a time Zafir had told her how much he loved and admired his esteemed parent, and one day hoped to display some of the wisdom and knowledge he was revered for himself.

'I'm sorry...I mean I'm sorry for your loss,' she added softly.

For a brief moment it looked as if the mistrust and suspicion in his eyes had lessened. But very quickly his expression was stony again, and it brought her firmly back to the present.

Raising his chin, he remarked, 'As I was saying, my position inevitably draws attention and not all of it is welcome. I am fully aware that those who are unscrupulous might try and steal from me from time to time.'

'Well, I'm not one of those.' Her brilliant blue eyes didn't hide her dismay. 'And there's nothing I want that I would be prepared to steal from *anyone*…certainly not anything material. If I couldn't buy it for myself then I'd just as soon forget it.'

'Then what is this urgent need you have to see me? The reason for all the messages you say you left at my office…messages that I never received?'

'I wanted to tell you about that in private. Somewhere we can speak freely.'

The expression on his face told Darcy that she was sorely testing him. His glance impatiently swept the room before returning to rest on her. 'This is private enough. You might not get another chance.'

'Why? Do you despise me so much that you can't bear the thought of seeing me again?'

Hearing the disturbing catch in her voice, Zafir

was alarmed. Could *any* man despise a woman who looked like she did?

He remembered the day she'd walked into his office, having been assigned to him as his PA. He had arranged that the bank's administrative manager would select someone for him, as it would be one less thing for him to do on his arrival from Zachariah, and the man who had selected Darcy from the pool of highly qualified secretaries the bank employed had assured him that she was one of the best. Having read her credentials, Zafir had agreed.

When he'd finally met her, his heart had stalled in surprise and pleasure. Her beauty had been the ethereal kind that romantic poets wrote the most exquisite accolades to…

All thoughts of work and the demanding schedule he'd had ahead of him had been instantly forgotten. Being a red-blooded, virile male, all he'd been able to think about was what it would be like to seduce her.

He'd never before experienced wanting a

woman as much as he'd wanted Darcy. Her shapely body and golden hair had captivated him from the very first. And it hadn't been only that. As he'd begun to get to know her he'd realised she had so many more attributes for him to admire. Kindness, generosity, and a ready smile no matter what she might be feeling. All came to her as easily as breathing, it had seemed.

A mere week later, having developed the habit of calling her in to his office more regularly than was strictly necessary—either on the pretext of taking dictation or to look over some 'important correspondence' with him—he had known he was falling in love...

Now, pushing his long hair back from his face, he immediately honed his gaze in on her tearful eyes. 'I don't despise you,' he said throatily. 'What is it you want to say? You may as well tell me now.'

Breathing out a sigh, he dropped down beside her on the bed, taking care not to jolt her elevated ankle. She immediately looked startled, then she quickly collected herself.

'All right, then. After you dismissed me…I—I found out that I was pregnant.'

There was a sudden deafening silence inside Zafir's head. The intensity of it, along with his racing heartbeat, tuned out any other sound. He likened it to standing in the vicinity of an explosion. When he finally composed himself, he considered the possibility that he might be dreaming. She had been *pregnant?* How could that be? He'd always made sure to protect her.

He was suddenly furious. 'Is this some kind of twisted joke you're playing on me, Darcy? I always took care to protect you from such an event. If you were pregnant, then the baby couldn't have been mine. Are you telling me that it was my *brother's?*'

The very idea made him feel sick to his stomach.

'I know you don't regard me very highly, but that's a vile accusation. The baby I had is *yours,*

Zafir…your *son*. That first time we were together neither of us were as careful as we should have been. I'd started taking the pill, but I hadn't been taking it long enough before we…before we spent the night together. Even though we'd planned it, everything happened so fast—don't you remember? We could barely contain our feelings.'

She meant that they hadn't been able to keep their hands off each other.

Even now the memory made him feel weak with longing. But at the back of his mind it suddenly nagged at him that in the throes of a desire as powerful and urgent as theirs had been he probably *hadn't* been as diligent with protection as he should have.

The evening they'd first become intimate had been when he'd taken her to one of the newest and most exclusive hotels in London. They had only stayed one night, but Zafir had made sure it was a night she would remember. He'd arranged for the lavish bed to be strewn with rose petals and the luxurious suite to be scented with a rare perfume that he'd had flown in from Zachariah. There had been nothing he wouldn't have done to help Darcy feel as if she was the centre of his universe...to show her that he was devoted to her happiness.

But later, when he'd learnt that she'd been cheating on him, his hopes that they would share the most joyous future together, that he would even go against tradition and make her his Queen, had shatteringly blown up in his face. And now she was telling him that he'd left her pregnant...

Zafir was glad he was sitting down. He felt as if he was in the middle of a storm whose power threatened to unbalance him no matter how hard he fought to stay upright. It wasn't the first time he'd reflected that he might have made the most terrible mistake when he'd let her go. But now, faced with the damning consequences of that decision—as well as wanting to somehow put things right—he needed to absorb the real possibility that he was a *father*. And if he was, he now had an heir.

His dearest wish had seemingly come to pass and he hadn't even known it. But the cruelty of doubt, of not being able to receive the news with any real confidence, still tormented him. Could he *really* have been such an utter fool back then when he'd fired her? Was he *really* the father of her son?

But as he examined her more closely he couldn't help but warm to the idea. 'Was I honestly so irresponsible as not to use protection the first time we made love?'

Darcy flushed. 'We were so crazy for each other that I don't think either of us had time to think about anything much…let alone be sensible.'

Remembering, Zafir was suffused by heat similar to that of a hot air current that swept across the desert sands. *No one could turn him on as she had.*

But he quickly returned to her story. 'Do you have *any* idea of what it means for someone in my position to have a son? It means that the ancient dynastic line of my forebears will continue. Nothing can bring greater satisfaction and purpose than that.'

His mind was racing with the implications of the news and how it was going to affect not just his life and his family's, but the people of Zachariah too.

'I'm glad that it's important to you. So, am I right in thinking that you want to be involved in our son's life?'

'If he *is* my son, then of course I want to be involved in his life. Did you not hear what I just said?'

'But…' Again, Darcy turned pink. 'What about your fiancée? Won't *she* want to have a say in any decision you make about that? It's surely going to come as a great shock to her that you have a son by someone else?'

Realising that he'd barely given his bride-to-be a thought since setting eyes on Darcy again, Zafir knew that he had to get out of marrying a woman he didn't love and had no chance of ever loving. He actually *welcomed* the idea of extricating himself from the arrangement.

Farrida came from a powerful Arabian family that was as wealthy and privileged as his own, and they'd known each other for years, but in truth she was a cold fish. She might be one of the most beautiful women in the kingdom, with an impeccable pedigree, but she had grown up utterly spoilt. Consequently she thought only of herself.

Zafir had only agreed to the marriage because—as his mother regularly reminded him—at some time or other he would have to produce an heir. He needed to put his duty first, and his union with Farrida would be considered highly advantageous by both families.

'Why don't you let *me* deal with that,' he replied tersely, 'and focus on getting your ankle better?'

'You must *know* I'm concerned about the fact you're getting married? It will have implications for me—and my son too. It's been a long, hard road with just my mum to help me with the childcare, so I can work and earn the money we need, and though I won't deny it would be helpful to have your support I don't want to risk losing Sami if you decide to sue for joint custody. Will you agree to his still living with *me*? When you talk about "dynastic lines", it worries me. I've wanted to tell you about our child for so long…but, as I said, I could never get through to you. When I read that you were getting married I knew it was more important than ever that you had the news.'

'And the boy… Sami…he is four now?'

'Yes.'

Darcy saw his glance soften for a moment as he seemed to take the time to reacquaint himself with her features. He followed it up with a lingering examination of her wheaten hair. He had always been fascinated by it… But she brought an abrupt halt to the memory when she started to remember how he'd loved to run his fingers through it.

It was perhaps fortunate when he quickly reverted to his previous less than friendly stance.

'I confess I am still having trouble believing all this, Darcy. I have plenty of reasons *not* to believe you…remember?'

His statement sent cold shivers scudding down her backbone. She saw that she still had to deal with his suspicion and mistrust.

'I never lied to you. I know you don't believe me, but it's true. You weren't the only one who was hurt by what happened. Not only did you think I was a liar and a cheat, but I also had to suffer the humiliation of being fired from my job as though…as though I was *worthless*. What happened wounded me more than you can possibly imagine. Let me go home, Zafir. *Please*,' she implored. 'I really do have to get back tonight. I give you my word that I'll be there should you want to discuss any plans concerning our son.'

He seemed to stare into her eyes for a very long time before he spoke, but she found no reassurance in his gaze…anything *but*. In those endless few seconds Darcy felt as if she was standing in front of a pitiless magistrate who was just about to condemn her to a prison cell for life. Was there *nothing* she could say that would move him?

'No matter how I feel personally about your predicament,' he remarked, 'in all conscience I cannot allow the hospital to discharge you tonight. You will have to stay here until tomorrow, when the doctor will re-examine you. After that, if I am satisfied they have done all that they can to aid your recovery, you can, of course, go home. But you can be sure I will be taking your details.'

'Why? Because you want to see Sami or because you still intend to prosecute me for trespass?'

Now her eyes *did* fill with tears.

His returning glance was unperturbed, and cool as iced water. 'To see my son, of course. I don't intend prosecution now I've learned the reason for your trying to break into the house.'

Sniffing, Darcy blotted her tears with the back of her hand. She bit her lip at his reference to her trying to break in. 'Good. But as to staying here for the night—I couldn't afford to, even if I was at death's door. Not *all* of us have money to burn like...'

'Like *me*? Is that what you were going to say?'

Shrugging his shoulders, as though it didn't disturb him one iota what she thought, Zafir started to walk away. But then he suddenly stopped dead and turned towards her.

Piercing her with eyes as black and mysterious as a moonless night, he breathed, 'You will not have to pay this particular bill, Darcy, *I* will. But do not doubt you will have to recompense me... one way or another.'

As the door of the room swung closed behind him she dropped her head back onto the pillows and stared wildly up at the ceiling. Her physical discomfort had eased, thanks to the pain medication kicking in, but she didn't know how she was going to relay the extraordinary events that had happened to her mother. And all because she'd finally taken matters into her own hands and recklessly sought Zafir out at his resplendent home...

* * *

Coming face to face with Darcy again did not help Zafir to sleep easily in his bed that night. The magic the woman weaved around him was like a drugging opiate that was impossible to resist, and when he was near her he felt like an addict on a recovery programme.

It was well over four years since he had seen her and at last he'd thought he'd got used to the idea that he would never see her again. But fate, it seemed, had had other plans. If it turned out to be the truth that he'd left her pregnant, then his whole life would change now that he had a son and heir.

Just as he was about to drift off to sleep he recalled the memory of her telling him how much she'd been hurt too—*more than he would ever know.* Now he knew what she'd meant—knew that she'd been pregnant by him when he'd fired her from her post—he felt like the cruellest tyrant imaginable for misjudging and abandoning her. But he still couldn't be sure she hadn't cheated on him with his brother, and until he was the idea would hang over him like Damocles' sword.

Waking early, Zafir hastily showered and dressed, then immediately instructed his chauffeur to drive him to the hospital. Half expecting Darcy to have somehow found a way of escaping, despite the fact that he had left Rashid guarding her door and she couldn't presently so much as put her foot to the floor, he couldn't suppress his relief when he saw her sitting on top of the hospital bed, fully dressed. She looked a little peaky, and she didn't seem best pleased to see him.

'Oh, it's you.'

Wanting to smile, he didn't. The situation was far too serious for any levity. 'Yes, it's me. Did you manage to get any sleep last night?'

'What do you care if I did or I didn't?'

'Don't be such a child.'

'I just want to get out of here and go home.'

She impatiently smoothed back a stray corngold strand of hair from her face, and her stare was defiant.

Zafir shook his head. 'You are going nowhere until I speak with the doctor—and even then not until you give me your phone number and address.'

That had sounded like a veiled threat, not something even *remotely* reassuring. Inside, Darcy's emotions clamoured. Wasn't it enough that he'd already stamped her heart into the ground and caused irreversible damage?

A mournful sigh escaped her. The reason she'd been so determined to confront him was because they had a son together...she should never forget that.

'I already *told* you I'd give them to you. I *want* to give you the chance to step up to your responsibilities—at the very least I thought you'd want that. And, more importantly, I want my son to know his father and likewise for you to get to know him and be proud of him.'

His tanned brow furrowed. Did she imagine

she saw the shadow of pain and regret in his glance?

'I would want all those things too,' he agreed soberly, '*if* he is indeed my son.'

Her stomach lurched at the idea he still didn't believe her.

'In any case, I intend to maintain contact with you. But right now I will go and tell the nurse we'd like to see the doctor.'

Darcy had no choice but to stay put. But when the time came she hoped she would be able to ring for a cab to take her home. She didn't want to resume relations with Zafir by feeling obligated. It was one thing having his support for Sami— if he gave it—and quite another having him lay down the law about what *she* did.

The question was would she be allowed to leave the hospital without any further intervention from him? It was hard to guess. The way her luck was going probably not.

When Zafir returned, she asked hopefully, 'Will I be discharged after I've seen the doctor?'

'We will soon find out. A nurse is coming to transport you to the examination room as we speak.'

A short while later Darcy nervously submitted to the doctor's examination of her swollen ankle. As Zafir watched the proceedings she saw his gaze was steely-eyed and serious.

Faint with worry, she mulled over the possible outcomes. What if they wanted to keep her here for another night? If that happened, what would she do? She was hardly in a position just to walk out. It went without saying that her mother would insist on visiting her, and if that happened by necessity she would have to bring Sami with her. It was a Saturday and the school week was over. But if Sami saw her in hospital she knew he would be distressed, seeing her incapacitated like this...

'Well, Ms Carrick, the outcome of your injury is presenting just as I expected. While it is very sore now, the ankle should heal beautifully if you take the proper care and rest. No doubt you must be relieved you didn't break any bones although you will still have to take some time off work.'

'Thank you. I *am* relieved that it's not as bad as I feared. All I want to do now is go home.'

'That is completely understandable, but first you must see our physiotherapist to be given some walking aids. When you have those, you may leave. The final thing I want to do is to tell you that you're a very fortunate young woman to have been aided by such a personage as the Sheikh of Zachariah himself.'

The doctor was hardly adept at concealing his curiosity as he peered at her more closely.

For his part, Zafir detected the man's too interested examination of Darcy's features straight away. Was he imagining that the delicate blonde with the angelic visage was his mistress? He didn't know why right then, but it seriously aggravated him.

'It won't be necessary for you to guide us to the physiotherapist, Dr Khan. A nurse can just as easily escort us.'

'As you wish, Your Highness.'

The doctor beamed and smiled, but Zafir didn't miss the brief flash of anxiety that flickered across the heavily lidded eyes. He could tell the man wasn't quite sure whether his services had pleased him or not, and no matter how admired he was in his field he wouldn't want to risk losing the Sheikh's patronage under any circumstances.

'I don't know *why* you thought I needed a wheel-chair, Zaf—Your Highness.' Colouring in embarrassment beneath the too astute scrutiny of Rashid, as he parked her chair by the side of his boss's gleaming black car, she privately cursed Zafir's insistence that she refrain from using his name because she was supposedly his *subordinate*.

The devastation she'd endured that day when he'd cruelly told her he didn't want anything to do with her any more was still able to wound her grievously. It wasn't unlike the symptoms of post-traumatic stress in that it was ever-present—it never went away. That being the case, she couldn't—*wouldn't* pretend that their association had been a casual one, no matter how high he'd risen in the meantime.

'It's not *that* difficult to manoeuvre a couple of walking sticks.'

The Sheikh's velvety dark brows came together in a forbidding frown. 'Why am I not surprised you would say that? I shouldn't have forgotten how stubborn you can be. Stop making a fuss and I will help you get into the car.'

All of a sudden he clicked opened the strap that secured her and, as Rashid held open the door, lifted her bodily into the car. Carefully arranging her bandaged ankle in the footwell, he briskly fastened her seatbelt and ordered his guard to take care of the crutches. Then, without even sparing her so much as a cursory glance, he sat down next to her. Rashid climbed in next to the driver.

Once more the sensual scent of exotic agar drifted beneath Darcy's nose, whilst the heat from her companion's body seemed to reach out to meld with her own. Pursing her lips, she wondered forlornly if anyone had recorded how fast a woman's heart beat when the love of her life acted as if it was a penance even to be in the same vicinity as her. Was there, in fact, a record for such a thing?

To stave off her distress, she blurted out, 'When I get home you don't have to come in with me. I can manage perfectly well using my walking aids.'

The man beside her turned slowly to survey her. 'Save your breath, Darcy, and listen to me. No matter how much you try to reassure me, I make no apologies for insisting that I accompany you. It would be remiss of me to take you home after your accident and then not come in with you to ensure you have everything you need and are safe.'

Now her heart beat hard for a different reason. He was going to meet their son for the very first time. What would he say? What would he do?

Sami was a sensitive little boy and was likely to be overwhelmed by the intimidating sight of Zafir unless she prepared him first. For all her quick thinking and bravado, how on earth was she going to deal with *that*?

CHAPTER THREE

DARCY HAD BOTH feared and longed for Zafir to meet his son, and it was hard to believe that at long last it was going to happen. Yet when the car pulled up outside the modest townhouse in the leafy London suburb where she lived, her fear about their meeting felt as if it might *choke* her.

She couldn't attest to being sure of him at all. What if he demanded custody of Sami in order to punish her because she hadn't told him about the pregnancy straight away? He was a powerful man with access to the best lawyers in the world. What was to stop him from suing her?

Moistening her dried lips, she nervously met his inscrutable dark gaze. 'You don't have to carry me into the house,' she said quickly. 'I'm happy to go in the wheelchair.'

'Good.'

For a few seconds he seemed amused, but she knew she shouldn't be fooled by some imagined sense of his warmth towards her. Not when he was so sure she'd wronged him.

The faithful Rashid remained waiting outside the car at a signal from his boss, and he watched and waited as His Highness helped her into the wheelchair. Steering her towards the front door, Zafir reached up to ring the bell.

Darcy felt sick to her stomach. It was only natural that she should anticipate the worst, she reasoned. This man was no longer her employer and one-time lover…he was now an unknown entity and a serious threat to all she held dear.

Quickly delving into her jacket pocket, she produced her key just in time. 'You don't need to ring the bell. I have my key.'

'Then give it to me and I'll let us in. Will there be anybody here to help you while your ankle heals?' His tanned brow furrowed, as if the notion that there might not be perturbed him.

Dropping the key into his palm, she scarcely felt able to reply. But in the next instant he'd wheeled her into the carpeted hallway and the only sound that greeted her was the ticking of the grandfather clock…the clock that had once been her dad's pride and joy. Other than that, the house was quiet.

'Sami and I live with my mum, but I think she must have gone out.'

Shutting the door behind them, he commented, 'I take it that means you don't have a husband?'

Planting himself firmly in front of her, the handsome Arabian folded his arms across his chest, leaving her in no doubt that he meant business and was going to find out the truth of her situation by whatever means necessary.

Gulping down an uneasy breath, she answered, 'No.' How could she tell him that she'd only ever wanted one man for her husband and that was him? 'There's no one in my life but Sami and my mother.'

'I can't pretend that I'm unhappy about that.'

His long-lashed black eyes focused on her intently. 'It could potentially complicate things if you were in a relationship.'

Knowing what he meant, she tightened her pale hands on the arms of the wheelchair. 'As it no doubt will when you marry this woman you're engaged to,' she said pointedly, unconsciously lifting her chin. 'If Sami goes to stay with you in the future I have to confess I'll be uncomfortable with the idea when I don't even know her. What's she like?'

'Her name is Farrida. She is from an important Zachariah family and her beauty and her intellect are much admired. We have known each other since we were children.'

The aloof manner in which he described his bride-to-be didn't tell Darcy very much about her at all—certainly not about the important things she wanted to know, such as her character and her values.

'Is she a warm and friendly person?' she

pressed. 'I suppose what I'm asking is, does she like children?'

His giving his intended a name, as well as listing attributes she definitely couldn't match, made the woman even more threatening to Darcy.

'And do...?' She hardly dared ask the next question. 'Do you love her?'

The glance Zafir returned to her was undeniably weary, as if the subject both bored and irritated him. 'As to whether she likes children or not—she knows that she's expected to produce heirs. This is not a love match. Arranged marriages are common practice amongst those with political power and wealth in my country. My family and hers typify that. Our destiny has always been to marry someone from a similar background.'

'So what you're saying is that you don't have a choice about who you marry?'

The smile he quirked was wry. 'My mother, the Dowager Queen, would not insist if the woman did not please me.'

'What do you mean by that?'

Unfolding his arms, he sighed, and his sigh was tinged with impatience. 'Surely *you*, of all women, must know what I mean? Have you so quickly forgotten how it was between us?'

The startling reminder was like a scythe slashing through her innards, because it was clear he was setting his sights on someone far above *her* background. Whether he would marry the well-connected beauty he spoke of or not, the woman surely had to be a much better bet than she had ever been.

She coughed to ease the tension that was cramping her throat. 'Do you think you could get me some water? The kitchen's just through that door.'

With a concerned expression, her companion briefly exited the room. He reappeared a few moments later with her drink. Once again the beguiling cologne he wore stirred the air, conjuring up potent imagery of a very different land whose history stretched back to the dawn of time.

'Do you need your medication?' he asked gruffly. 'I have it here.'

He gave her the painkillers, along with the glass of water.

'Thanks.' Pressing the foil packet with trembling fingers, Darcy emptied a couple of capsules into her hand. Then she hurriedly swallowed them down with the drink, all the while aware that her one-time lover watched her avariciously, almost like a hawk about to bear down on his prey.

'That's better,' she remarked, for no other reason than that it was something to break the silence that had fallen.

'Even though we are no longer lovers,' Zafir suddenly declared, 'if I choose not to marry Farrida, and it can be proved that Sami is indeed my son, there *is* a way you can repay me for not telling me sooner that you were carrying my child when you left the bank.'

Darcy bristled. 'When I was *forced* to leave the bank, do you mean?'

Unperturbed, the steady black eyes held her gaze. 'That is a conversation for later…not now. Concerning your repayment—I have a solution. I want you to replace Farrida by agreeing to become my wife.'

'*What?* You can't be serious.'

Relieving her of the glass of water, he put it down on a nearby bookshelf. When he turned back, a muscle flinched tellingly at the side of a breathtakingly carved cheekbone.

'One convenient bride is much the same as another. Except that *you* have one important thing in your favour, Darcy. It seems that you have already given me the requisite heir.'

She flinched as though struck, but knew he wouldn't be displaying any remorse for stating things so bluntly. And she was right. All she saw in the silken black orbs was an intimidating mockery that told her it was utterly pointless to argue.

Praying she could remain calm, even though her heart already felt as if it might burst, she said, 'Do you *really* think that I'd marry you after what happened between us? Our relationship didn't work out because you didn't trust me, Zafir. Instead, you believed the despicable lies your brother told you, and didn't see that the sickening incident in that office was nothing but a set-up, engineered to discredit me. You never even gave me a chance to tell you how difficult he was making things for me at work. Straight away you thought me faithless!'

Taking a deep breath in to compose herself, she continued.

'Xavier had been harassing me for months leading up to the day it happened. He was getting more and more frustrated by my lack of interest in him and he wanted to pay me back for it.'

At that moment the sense of abandonment and grief that she'd carried for all these years dramatically reached its peak and spilled over. The feeling was akin to being caught in a wild, untamed storm that had drenched her and now it was too late to escape from being drowned… All she could do was pray it would end soon and that her life would return to some sense of normality.

'Then you heartlessly fired me.'

'And you expect me to believe that?'

'I don't tell lies—especially when it concerns something as important as this. Sami is your son, Zafir. Do you intend to punish me even more than you've done already for telling you the truth about it?'

She was already aware that the knowledge he had a son would change *everything* for him. He had often told her the importance of having a male heir in his culture.

'We made love in the heat of the moment that first time and I'd only just started taking the pill. I didn't have time to properly protect myself, and…if you remember…nor did you.'

'And you didn't consider having an abortion?'

His voice sounded like a husk of its former self, and his glistening brow attested to the tumult of emotion he must be feeling.

'I wouldn't ever have done such a thing.'

'Why not, isn't it common practice in the West the acceptable cost of having your fun and not paying for it?'

She grimaced. 'Whether it is or it isn't, in my experience no woman makes that decision lightly. And, personally, I believe that life is too precious to destroy.'

Frowning, he said tersely, 'So do I—but yet again you have probably told me a duplicitous story. More likely than not, I am not the *only* man you have been intimate with. You forget that there were rumours about the way you conducted yourself around men at the bank. Not least of all my own brother.'

'And did you bother to check out any of these claims? Instead of automatically believing them to be true? And just because your brother is who he is, it doesn't mean that you can trust him. Xavier lies as easily as he breathes, and you don't do yourself any favours being so ready to believe him.'

'Enough!'

Stepping towards her in a moment of white-hot fury, Zafir clenched his fist. His expression was fierce, and Darcy could tell she'd really upset him.

In those electrifying few seconds she wanted to die. No woman could endure what she had in a relationship and then expect things to somehow magically turn around for the better...could they?

But thankfully in the next instant, as if realising he had come perilously close to losing control, he seemed to gather himself.

'Whatever the outcome of this meeting, you can be certain of one thing—' he vowed ominously.

He wasn't able to finish whatever it was he'd been about to say, but she sensed it wasn't good. The very second he was about to break her heart again she heard the sound of a key in the door, along with the sound of childish laughter.

Her family had returned.

'It's my mum and Sami.'

'What?'

Now it was her turn to leave *him* hanging. Eagerly she steered her wheelchair towards the living room door. Just as she reached it, her family did too.

'Mummy, you're back! Are you feeling better now?'

'Much better, my darling, all the more for seeing *you*.'

Affectionately gathering the little boy with dusty blond curls and big brown eyes into her arms, Darcy pressed her lips into his hair, inhaled his familiar musky small-boy scent and forgot that Zafir was even there. All was right with her world because her son was safely home.

'Nanny bought me a new football, Mummy. It's a Chelsea one.' He held up the shiny carrier bag he was clutching for her to see.

Full of excitement, he glanced across his mother's shoulder just then and saw Zafir. His slim little body went rigid. The man's impressive physique and attire might be seen as intimidating by *anyone*, but to a small boy with a head full of adventures—mostly featuring bloodthirsty pirates and sword-wielding warriors—Zafir looked nothing less than *awesome*.

Stepping back a little, Sami croaked, 'Who are *you*?'

Darcy manoeuvred the wheelchair around so that she could catch the expression on her ex-lover's face when he answered. She hardly dared breathe.

At the same time, understandably anxious to know what was going on, her mother, Patricia, leant down to her and whispered, 'Are you all right, love? I didn't see an ambulance outside. How did you get home?'

Having not yet related to her the full story about her accident, Darcy murmured softly, 'This gentleman brought me. I used to work for him. We—we recently met up again and he kindly brought me back from the hospital.'

She hoped that would suffice for now. But as her gaze lit on Zafir she couldn't help but be anxious about what he would say next.

Taking her by surprise, he dropped down to his haunches, his gaze growing noticeably warmer as he addressed the small boy. 'Your name is Sami?'

It wasn't hard to see that Sami was fascinated by him.

'Yes.'

'It is a fine name and it suits you well.'

'It's my dad's middle name, and my granddad's too, but I've never met them.'

'I'm sure you would make them both very proud if they were to meet you.'

With his beloved father now dead, it wasn't possible that such a meeting could ever take place, and Zafir sensed a renewed sting of grief for the man who hadn't just been a wise father and friend, but his mentor too. 'A king amongst kings,' his mother often declared when talking about him.

Zafir's limbs felt like lead. Suddenly mute, he had the disturbing sense of being in a most fantastical dream, where nothing was quite real any more. He looked at the boy. Could he really be his son? A wave of feeling gripped him. Hot on the heels of his initial doubt, a fierce hope was kindling. It was a feeling of the most incredible *joy*…the kind of joy that perhaps visited a person once in a lifetime, and then only if they were lucky.

As he studied the boy more closely his stomach must have flipped half a dozen times. Was it true? Zafir couldn't deny that he saw distinct similarities to himself. Even though the child's hair was almost as fair as freshly churned butter, and a million miles away from being dark, the deep brown almond-shaped eyes, the budding aquiline nose and full lips might have been sculpted by the same divine hand that had created his own. Add to that the ethereal loveliness of his mother, the boy was exceptionally beautiful…eye-catching, in fact.

That brought him back to the woman in question. Seeing Darcy again was a shock that nothing on this earth could have prepared him for, and he was still feeling a kind of dizziness around her—similar to that of a man whose drink had been spiked with some kind of opiate. To contemplate the revelation that their brief, passionate affair had created a child was astounding. The implications were enormous if it turned out to be true.

Even so, at the forefront of his mind burned the question *why* hadn't she found some way to get the news to him when she'd discovered she was pregnant? She'd said that she'd left messages. But he'd never received any of them.

Zafir's chest grew uncomfortably tight. He might be reflecting that Darcy could have got the news to him if she'd *wanted* to...but after being coldly rejected by him and dismissed from her job she had no longer trusted him. Why should she have when he had believed his brother's telling of events over hers?

In her defence, at the time she'd insisted that Xavier had deliberately engineered the compromising scene in which Zafir found them because—as she'd said—he'd wanted to pay her back for holding out on him. He'd been pestering her with his unwanted attentions for weeks, she'd told him, but she hadn't had the courage to report him. Not because she was a coward, but because the situation was clearly a sensitive one. How could she accuse Xavier of sexually harassing her and expect to be believed when his family was as eminent and powerful as theirs was? she'd asked him. Not only that, they were her employers too...

Zafir had found himself presented with one of the worst dilemmas of his life.

Now, not for the first time, he felt sick at the thought that he might have made a terrible mistake in wrongly accusing Darcy. But no sooner had the notion entered his head than he knew it wouldn't be wise to jump to conclusions.

This time he would force himself to take a more measured approach in finding out the truth. And to that end he would insist on taking a paternity test. If it turned out that he *was* the father of her child, then and *only* then would he make the knowledge official and assume his full responsibilities. But for now he wouldn't allow his personal feelings to take precedence—even though his heart had joyously leapt at the idea he might at long last have a son and heir.

Like a moth that on some level must know it would get burned by the flame it couldn't resist, once again he found himself drawn to the blonde sitting quietly in her wheelchair. He got slowly to his feet. Even though she was understandably under par after her accident, her beauty was still radiant. The colour of her eyes was akin to a rare blue topaz, and they dazzled him like diamonds, whilst her pretty mouth made him remember with longing what it had felt like to touch his lips to hers. He had never known a pleasure like it.

The first time Zafir had met her he'd instantly thought her the most beguiling creature he'd ever seen, and had likened her to the stunning flaxen-haired princess from one of the old Arabian tales he'd heard from his nursemaid as a child. The legend went that whenever this princess caught a man in her gaze his heart and soul would be pledged to her for ever.

As if suddenly aware that the silence between them had stretched on too long, Darcy turned to the attractive older woman by her side and addressed her. Zafir had already assumed she must be her mother. Her tinted blonde hair must have once had the same golden hue as her daughter's, he guessed.

In a determined tone, Darcy announced, 'By the way, Mum, I didn't introduce you. This is His Royal Highness Sheikh Zafir el-Kalil of Zachariah.' She flicked him a glance that left him in no doubt that she was on her guard.

His abdomen clenched as though he'd been sucker-punched as Zafir chillingly recalled his instinctive urge to lash out when she'd accused his brother of being a liar. Whether blood was thicker than water or not, he'd broken his own strict code of conduct in reacting like that. As Allah was his judge, he would rather cut off his hand than hurt a single hair on her head…

'And this is my mother, Patricia Carrick, Your Highness.'

'I am honoured to make your acquaintance, Mrs Carrick.' Having been raised always to respect his elders, in the midst of his turmoil he somehow found a smile.

'And this is a privilege *I* never expected, Your Highness.' Her mother couldn't help giving an awkward little curtsey that made her daughter flush.

Her mother was transfixed by the man's attention.

Then, what female *wouldn't* be, no matter how old she was? Darcy mused.

'I know that Darcy once worked for an Arabian bank whose owners had a royal bloodline, but that was quite some time ago now…in fact a few months before she had Sami.'

It was as if Patricia had just pulled the pin on a hand grenade, and the room fell preternaturally quiet. Reminding herself of the reason that Zafir had brought her home from the hospital in the first place, Darcy found herself staring at the neat white bandage taped round her ankle.

Had her mother not yet put two and two together? If not, then surely it was only a matter of time before she did.

Knowing that the last thing she felt like facing was confrontation, Darcy sought to steer her away from the subject. Lifting her hand to conceal a fake yawn, she made her voice apologetic. 'I'm sorry, Mum, but I'm really feeling quite tired, and I'm sure His Highness has to get on. It's been quite an ordeal. I think I'll go and have a lie-down in a minute, if you could watch Sami?'

'Of course, dear. Why don't you let me take him upstairs while you say goodbye to His Highness? Then you can take a nap.'

'Thanks.'

His glance temporarily alighting on the older woman, Zafir made a polite bow. 'It has been an honour meeting you, Mrs Carrick.'

'And you, Your Highness.'

Putting out his hand, he briefly laid it on the child's small shoulder and bestowed upon him a warmly unguarded smile that made his mother's heart stall.

'It has been a delight and a pleasure to meet you too, Sami,' he told him. 'I hope we shall be able to see each other again soon.'

'Cool!' he replied, with the happy grin that he generally reserved for his best friend, Ben, at school.

Darcy mused that her son didn't easily give his trust to anyone. Had some deep inner instinct already made him bond with the man who was his father?

Her teeth grazing at her lip, she watched him run out to the hall staircase, followed more slowly by his grandmother. In just a few short moments she heard his footsteps race excitedly into his room. No doubt he would be playing eagerly with his toys.

CHAPTER FOUR

THE AIR STIRRED behind her and Darcy realised that Zafir had moved to stare out at the postage-stamp-sized garden beyond the French doors. He must think it ridiculously small compared to his own generous acreage. If it weren't for the injury she'd sustained, she would hardly believe that she'd dared to climb his garden wall. But 'needs must as the Devil drives', she thought. Facing the very *worst* of demons wouldn't faze her if it helped ensure her son's well-being and security.

'You don't have to stay any longer,' she told him, her voice sounding strained even to her own ears.

'Oh, but I do,' he insisted, turning to look at her. There was a flash of steel in his eyes. 'There are still a few things we need to discuss.'

'I thought we'd covered most things.'

'Don't play games with me. I want a straight answer from you. Was I really your *only* lover at the time, Darcy?'

Her skin prickled with indignant heat. 'You accused me once before of sleeping with other men because you listened to office gossip. It was a contemptible lie then and it's still a lie now. Do you imagine I'd ever want to see you again if it wasn't for a very good reason? You hurt me so badly, Zafir, that's it's a wonder I could ever hold my head up again. The only reason I wanted to make contact with you is because of Sami.'

'You say you tried to reach me, but how *hard* did you try?'

Once again he rubbed salt into her wounds with the disbelief that sounded in his voice. Had the faith and trust he'd used to have in his ability to make good judgements been *so* diminished by his brother's lies?

Disconsolately, she shook her head. 'Only the

person who took my calls and deals with your post can tell you that.'

'Are you saying it was my personal secretary?'

She flinched, because that had used to be *her* role. 'I can only presume that's who it was—or maybe someone who obeyed her instructions?'

Darcy saw him swallow hard.

'Make no mistake. I will be making my own investigations into the matter'

'I shouldn't have let our association become more personal when I came to work for you, however strong my feelings were at the time. But I can't regret it because it gave me my son. He's the only good thing that's come out of that whole sorry episode. Now all I want is for us to have some peace and for our lives to return to normal.'

'Then let me tell you *this.*'

He moved across to her in a flash and, with a rustle of the luxuriant robes he wore over black jeans and cut-off leather boots, dropped down in front of her, one hand possessively trapping hers as it rested on the wheelchair arm. His touch was like being exquisitely burned, and Darcy gasped.

'The first thing that's going to happen tomorrow is that I'm going to take a paternity test with Sami. If it turns out that I am indeed his father, then wheels will very quickly be put into motion to do what is right by him.'

'What do you mean?'

A muscle in the side of his sculpted cheek flinched. 'I mean I will let my family know that I have sired a son and heir and, to that end, I will be returning home to Zachariah to present him.'

'Now, wait just a minute. Do you honestly think I'm going to let you leave the country with him? Let me remind you that he's *my* son too, Zafir. I'm the one who's raised him all these years, not you.'

'And whose fault is that, *habibi*?' His hand firming more tightly round hers, he tugged her towards him. 'You tell me that you tried to reach me—but until I find out if that's true the fact is that I had no idea you'd had a child. If the paternity test turns out to prove without a doubt that he is my flesh and blood, you should understand that there are going to be some serious consequences.'

'Are you *threatening* me?' Shocked by his vehemence, Darcy turned cold. 'There are laws in this country that—'

But she never got the chance to say anything else because suddenly his hands were firmly gripping her waist and he was impelling her towards him. In the next instant he possessively crushed her lips under his. It was a passionate, bruising kiss that was full of fury as well as blistering desire.

Back when she'd first known him the combustible fusion that had driven them into bed that very first time had been white-hot and charged, but even then she'd only succumbed to being intimate with him because she'd been falling in love with him.

Their lovemaking had culminated in her falling pregnant. But never at any time had she considered aborting her baby because their relationship had ended so disastrously. Right from the start Darcy had had an incontrovertible sense that it was her *destiny* to have his child.

But she'd never experienced the taste of punishing anger on his lips until now. It was clear she had to suppress the need and desire that was feverishly charging through her and somehow find the strength to push him away. She should never forget that this man had betrayed her when he'd chosen to believe his brother's lies about her, and that it had cost her much more than just the loss of her job. How could she ever trust him again?

With her eyes brimming with tears and her breath tight, Darcy stared back into the Arabian's stunningly carved visage and for a moment was reassured in her decision to hold back. There wasn't the least bit of remorse in his expression. In fact he seemed infuriated that she'd curtailed the embrace. His own breath was coming in short sharp gasps and he raised the back of his hand to wipe his mouth, as if to wipe away her taste.

Then, with noticeably less care than he'd previously exhibited, Zafir pushed her back down into the wheelchair.

'You are no longer going to have everything your way, Darcy. Now that I am back in your life things are very definitely going to change. I will pick you and the child up tomorrow morning, to go to the clinic. In the meantime you should rest as much as possible and get some of your strength back. Don't lock the front door when I'm gone— I'm going to get your walking aids from the car.'

'You're behaving as if you already know the outcome of the test. You surely wouldn't go to all this trouble if you suspected for even a second that you *aren't* Sami's father…that he's someone else's.'

'When it comes to women I am as liable as the next man to being prey to feminine wiles, and in this particular case I want to be absolutely sure I am not being led astray. In my country, do you know how vital it is for its rulers to father sons? We are a rich but small kingdom, and if we don't procreate we run the risk of being taken over by larger tribes in neighbouring kingdoms. I can't emphasise more strongly than that how vital it is that I make certain that your claims are true.'

On that note he left the house, and she heard his deep bass tones carry on the air as he talked to his bodyguard, Rashid. The enormity of the situation washed over Darcy like encroaching floodwater and her body shivered convulsively.

If someone had predicted to her that one day Zafir would come back into her life and want to claim his son, she'd honestly have thought them deluded. Astonishingly, he'd proved her wrong. Her lips were still tingling where his had so passionately left their imprint and she knew they were likely to be contused.

Tentatively touching her fingertips to the softly swollen flesh, she sighed. Even though she knew his visit was no imagined fantasy—that it was electrifyingly *real*—it still felt as though she was in a dream when he appeared in the room again, her walking aids tucked carefully under his arm. He set them down by the sofa.

Every time she was confronted by the sight of him—in spite of his obvious mistrust and the grief he'd left her with—her hopes soared that even if he couldn't bring himself to love her again, as he once had, perhaps he would genuinely want to be a proper father to his son? Right then, she refused to think about his engagement.

'I will leave them here, at the end of the couch, so you can reach them when you need to get up.'

'Thanks.'

'You will not be able to manage to do things on your own for a while, until your injury heals. I'm thinking of hiring a nurse for you.'

A sense that events were taking on a distinct life of their own and running away with her gave Darcy the shivers. She needed to impress upon him the fact that she still had a mind of her own.

Imbuing firmness into her tone, she replied, 'That won't be necessary. My mum is with me, remember?'

Zafir frowned, 'Ah, yes, she lives with you.'

'Yes. She looks after Sami for me when I'm at work, and she'll take care of things until I'm up and about again.'

'And where, may I ask, do you work these days?'

'I work for a temping agency rather than a single employer. The jobs are quite varied and I like that. It also gives me the flexibility I need to be at home whenever Sami is ill.'

'Resourceful as ever, I see.' The coal-black eyes glimmered thoughtfully.

'I've had to be. Obviously I need to earn money to keep us and pay my rent.'

'You do not own this property?'

'You're joking! Mum and I rent it together. Have you *any* idea how much I'd need to put down as a deposit in order to get a mortgage?' A warm flush swept across her cheeks and she knew she sounded defensive. 'Anyway, I'm really tired now and I need to rest. I'll see you in the morning.'

Zafir nodded. 'I will be here for you at nine-fifteen, to ensure we get to the clinic on time. I advise you to rest that ankle and get to bed early. Where will you sleep tonight? Here on the couch?'

'Yes, probably.'

'Whatever you do, do not attempt the stairs. Have you a downstairs cloakroom?'

She shouldn't be surprised that although he came from a world of privilege he was automatically considering the practicalities of her situation, but she was. 'Yes, I do.'

'Good. Then I'll see you and the child tomorrow.'

Making one last sweeping examination of her, as if to satisfy himself that she could be trusted to keep her word, he turned round and left.

Even though the situation was nowhere near to being conclusive yet, Zafir's first thought when he got home was to ring Farrida and let her know that their marriage was off…that she should no longer consider herself engaged to him.

She wouldn't take the news at all calmly, and would probably rant and rail at him, listing all the reasons why he was a fool to break his pledge—not least of all because their families had wanted their union since they were children and he would never find another woman more suitable than her.

However, he sensibly decided to postpone the call until he'd had the results of the test from the clinic. Farrida could wait...

That night, to while away the inevitably tense hours that ensued, Zafir played cards with Rashid. The man was a lousy card-player, but couldn't be faulted for his enthusiasm. However, it was hard to concentrate on the game when his fertile mind kept taking him down paths he was wary of following.

There were too many as yet unresolved issues for his liking—too many for him to be confident of specific outcomes. But the following day might present the most important revelation of his life so far—that he was the father of the handsome boy whom he'd only discovered existed yesterday.

Although the mere idea of his having a son was unquestionably wonderful, the fact that he hadn't even known of his existence for over four years grievously wounded him. Had the prospect of seeing him again been so unpalatable to her that Darcy had delayed letting him know she was pregnant? Or had she feared what he might do?

He had fired her because he'd found her in his brother's arms at the office, for goodness' sake! The evidence against her could hardly have been more damning.

Yet it still nagged at him that he'd made the most terrible mistake. Why? Because it had become increasingly clear that Xavier had a worrying predilection for indulging in indiscriminate liaisons, and a year after Darcy had gone he'd discovered that he was conducting an intimate relationship with one of the bank's married secretaries—even after being warned that any more compromising behaviour would absolutely not be tolerated.

Zafir had ordered him straight back to Zachariah as punishment, telling him not to return until he could prove he had changed for the better. He would not allow the family's good name to be dragged through the mud. In his opinion Xavier had been far too indulged growing up and this was the result. Consequently he was going to have to demonstrate much more exemplary behaviour and become a man the family was truly proud of before he could even *think* about claiming the generous inheritance left to him by their father…

It was a quarter past nine on the dot the next morning when his chic and luxurious car arrived to collect Darcy and her son. She was clearly insistent on using her crutches, and Sami walked protectively beside her to the car.

Zafir owned to a warm burst of pride that the boy was behaving like a real gentleman at such a tender age. *Some might say that royal blood will out*, he thought, smiling. But although he was charmed by him, his gaze kept gravitating to Darcy.

Today she was wearing a simple navy blue skirt with a fitted matching jacket. The mid-length skirt displayed her shapely knees and calves to perfection, but it was her heart-stopping features and the pretty flaxen hair resting against her nape in a neat ponytail that inevitably drew his attention.

He could hardly look away, even though he immediately sensed that she wasn't feeling remotely sociable. She was wearing make-up, but the light application couldn't disguise the fact that she was porcelain-pale. Was she nervous about the outcome of the test this morning, in case it proved that he *wasn't* Sami's father?

He deliberately stopped the thought dead in its tracks. One step at a time, he told himself.

When they arrived, a trim uniformed nurse with chestnut hair met them at the entrance of the clinic and led them inside to the suite where the tests would be conducted. As the automatic glass doors swished open Zafir situated himself protectively between Darcy and the boy, as if he had already acknowledged that he was head of the family.

'Do you think this will take very long?' she asked him, stopping for a moment as if to take a breather from the effort of using the crutches.

There was a slight sheen of sweat on her brow. Concerned, he gently pressed her shoulder. 'Why? Is it too much for you to stand? I can carry you into the examination room, if you like?'

'No. I'll be all right.'

Her lips formed a tight, reluctant little smile that told him she was far from being 'all right' and he frowned. 'Are you nervous about the outcome of the test?'

'What have I to be nervous about? I've always known the truth—right from day one. It's *you* who suspects I might be lying.'

As if he'd been stung, his hand dropped away.

He glanced across at Sami. The last thing he wanted to do was make the child fear him, should he sense there was tension between him and his mother. If the test revealed what his heart willed it to then his greatest desire was that he and Sami would start to build a good relationship—the kind of loving, mutually respectful relationship that Zafir had enjoyed with his own father.

'Your Highness... Ms Carrick and Master Carrick...please follow me and we'll get the paternity test underway.'

The trim nurse who had met them at Reception smiled warmly and led them into a room that, with its ecru couches and colourful cushions, clearly aimed to be as inviting as possible in order to put clients at their ease. But the indelible aroma of antiseptic pervaded the atmosphere and it was impossible to disguise its purpose.

The three of them took their seats and straight away Zafir noticed that Darcy avoided meeting his eyes. Instead she concentrated her gaze on her son. As he privately acknowledged his fear of the test's outcome the capacity for speech seemed to desert him. Never had so much depended on the results of what was a fairly routine test these days, and he found his gut clenching as if to ward off a blow.

For a couple of minutes he fiddled with the band of his thick gold signet ring, just for something to do. Thankfully, they didn't have to wait long before a clinician arrived. The young twenty-something man, who was already losing his hair, took the requisite cell samples by swabbing the insides of their cheeks with cotton buds which were then put into a container, sealed and labelled with their names.

'All done,' he said brightly, surveying them closely with his keen-eyed glance, but being careful not to seem intrusive. 'In twelve hours' time I'll be able to give you the results. You can ring me on this number at about ten tonight, Your Highness.'

Taking a small white card out of his pocket, he handed it to Zafir.

'Are there any further questions?'

Zafir wanted to reply *yes*. How were they supposed to while away twelve hours and not succumb to the most unbearable tension?

As if reading his mind, the clinician—his voice still indomitably cheerful—said, 'I'll take that as a no, then. As you probably know, Hyde Park isn't very far from here, if you feel like taking a walk. There's a good café there, where you can get drinks and food. You can also feed the ducks that swim on the lake. Do you have a wheelchair with you, Ms Carrick?'

Clearing her throat, as if her voice had gone rusty after several minutes' lack of use, Darcy glanced at Zafir then quickly looked away again. 'His—His Highness has one in the car for me.'

'Good. Then I suggest that you go and enjoy the day and try not to worry.'

With Sami happily holding her hand as she rode in the wheelchair—Zafir manoeuvring her and Rashid dutifully following behind at a suitably discreet distance, but still within earshot—Darcy started to relax a little.

The clinician's idea about going to the park had been a good one. There was nothing like a dose of fresh air, the sight and scent of recently rained-on grass and a plethora of English oak trees to help raise the spirits, she thought. Add to that her beautiful little son, skipping cheerfully alongside her, and his equally beautiful, often brooding father wheeling her, in those precious few hours before their immediate future was decided on she could hardly have wished for more...

They made their way towards the wide glinting lake in the afternoon sunshine, and Sami rushed ahead when he spied the small flotilla of ducks converging at the waterside.

'Mummy, there are *loads* of ducks here!' he called out excitedly.

Zafir shouted back. 'Don't get too near to the water, Sami. Wait for me and your mother.'

'All right... But I only want to talk to them, Your Highness.'

In response, Zafir threw his head back and laughed heartily. The sound raised Darcy's flesh to goosebumps, it was so joyful.

She twisted in her chair to look up at him. 'What's so funny?'

'He is so polite and well mannered…a real credit to you. Who told him to call me *Your Highness*? Did you?'

Returning his smile, she dimpled. 'No. I expect it was my mum—either that or he heard her refer to you as that.'

'Like I said—he is a credit to you, Darcy.'

For a long moment she allowed herself to bathe in the undeniable warmth of his lingering glance, and she almost forgot that there had ever been any disagreement between them. But even then she knew not to hope for too much. So many things were still unsettled.

Just as they reached the lakeside, and saw Sami happily chattering to the ducks, they noticed a fit and spry elderly couple with tans like mahogany moving purposefully towards them.

The woman called out. 'Is that your little boy? I'm guessing he must be. You can see where he inherits his good looks. He's a real mixture of you both, if you don't mind my saying? By the way, that's a magnificent costume you're wearing, sir. Are you in the theatre?' she asked curiously, staring at Zafir.

After a wry glance towards Darcy first, he looked back and answered, 'I fear you have found me out. I should have changed when rehearsals ended, but my son was eager to feed the ducks'

'Oh, my—do you mind if I get a picture of you?'

Fully expecting her companion instantly to say no, Darcy was amazed when Zafir agreed.

'Why don't you take one of all of us?' he suggested, standing next to her with his hand resting possessively on her shoulder and at the same time calling out to Sami to come and join them.

One photo had turned into three by the time the American couple said their effusive goodbyes and departed, by which time Sami declared that he was hungry.

'Then we should go to the café and have a sandwich. We can save some bread to feed the ducks,' Zafir suggested.

'Can we have cake too?'

'But of course.'

'Cool.' With a delighted grin the little boy ran to Zafir's side and slipped his hand into his as if it was the most natural thing in the world for him to do… In fact, as if he had been doing it all his life…

CHAPTER FIVE

SAMI FELL ASLEEP in the car and, with her arm protectively tucked around him, so did Darcy. An undeniable sense of 'rightness' filled Zafir as he observed the pair, and the more he looked the stronger the feeling grew.

Other than the very first time he'd set eyes on his stunning blue-eyed secretary, he'd never had such a powerful sense of something significant happening—something that he couldn't control. Something that might possibly change his life...

He had always been restless by nature, too hungry to settle for what he deemed the 'ordinary' aspirations of others. But coming from royal lineage meant that somewhere along the line it was essential that he marry and have children. It had been playing on his mind for quite some time now, and his mother regularly got in touch to remind him about it and his agreement to Farrida. But she was the *last* woman he wanted to think about now...

There was still a fire in him to try and make a positive difference to those less fortunate, and he would continue to do so in whatever way he could, but having a loving relationship and the joy of a family of his own had suddenly become the most important thing of all. Was it seeing Darcy again that had made the idea seem more urgent?

He had never forgotten their love affair, and nor had he got over it... That period in his life had been an incredible time out of time, and for a while he had been joyously lost in his feelings for her. If she *had* betrayed him with his brother, as he'd thought, he wouldn't be able to forgive her easily. Yet he couldn't deny that he was desperate to know if her son *was* his.

The time when he'd receive the test results from the clinic couldn't come quickly enough.

Moving suddenly, Darcy yawned and sat up. A few strands of silky blonde hair had worked loose from her ponytail, and as the sunlight zeroed in on them through the window beside her they seemed to crackle with electricity.

'Are we nearly home?'

For a moment those matchless blue eyes that were highlighted by dark gold lashes stopped him in his tracks. It was like glancing into the most extraordinarily still mountain lake. The bewitching appeal that had hypnotised him from the very first hadn't decreased in the slightest. In fact it had become even more mesmerising.

Snapping out of the near trance he'd fallen into, he sucked in a breath to compose himself. 'We are just approaching your house...look.'

'What a relief.'

'You must be tired. Let me help you.'

'It would help me more if you could carry Sami.'

'Gladly.'

When they reached the living room it was to

find Darcy's mother waiting. When she saw Zafir her smile was awkwardly deferential, but she immediately lifted the still drowsy Sami from out of his arms.

'He's probably had a bit too much excitement for one day, Your Highness. Darcy told me you were heading off to the park when she rang. I'll take him up to his room and read to him for a while. If he falls asleep I'll come back down and make you both a nice cup of tea.'

The couple were silent as Patricia disappeared upstairs, but it wasn't by any means an *easy* silence. The two of them were both behaving as though they were wary of saying or doing the wrong thing. The situation was a veritable powder keg that might blow up in their faces at any time, and they both knew it…

Chewing down on the inside of her cheek, Darcy gingerly lowered herself onto the couch. She was grateful when her companion immediately stepped forward to relieve her of the crutches and lean them against a chair, but she *wasn't* grateful that the tantalising scent of his cologne too easily had the power to scramble her brain. Plus, her injured ankle had developed the same nagging ache as a persistent sore tooth, and she couldn't suppress her irritation. Add to that the stress of going for a paternity test to prove to her son's father that he *was* the one responsible for siring him—surely it would be one stress too many in *anyone's* book?

'You don't have to stay for a cup of tea,' she declared suddenly. 'Let's not pretend this is some kind of fond reunion, when we both know it's anything *but*. My mum was just being polite.'

'And clearly you don't feel the same need? To be polite, I mean?' He crossed his arms over his chest, his black eyes glinting disapprovingly.

'I can be as polite as the next person. But that doesn't mean I have to act pleased that you're here. If I hadn't had that fall at your house we wouldn't even be having this conversation. In all this time you've never bothered to find out what happened to me. You sacked me from a job I loved and probably didn't lose an ounce of sleep wondering how I would manage to survive. And I don't suppose it ever crossed your mind that you might have left me pregnant?'

At last. To say what was true was like puncturing a painful cyst that had troubled her for too long. Although upsetting, she was glad of the release of expressing her pent-up emotion. Even more so because she'd been certain that she'd never get the chance…

The expression on Zafir's handsome, strong-boned face was stunned. There was a visible tremor in his hand when he lifted it to push back a swathe of rich dark hair.

'As we are on the subject, did it ever cross *your* mind how I must have felt when I found you in the arms of my brother?'

White-hot rage such as she'd never felt before erupted inside Darcy. 'As I told you at the time—and again the other day—it was a set-up! If you'd had any *real* feeling for me you would have seen that. Xavier had been plaguing me for weeks. When you came into the office, just as he grabbed me and kissed me, I knew by the look in your eyes that you hadn't seen the triumphant smirk on his face. You wouldn't even give me the chance to put my side of the story. Instead you condemned me. It was as though what we had shared meant *nothing* to you.'

The interminable silence that ensued made Darcy feel as if she was walking barefoot on broken glass... Already she felt as if she was inwardly bleeding.

When it came, Zafir's reply was surprisingly frank.

'If what you say is indeed true, then I have undoubtedly paid the price for my actions. Not only did I not know that I might have fathered a child, but I might have hurt his mother beyond measure...a woman I'd come to care for and respect...'

He looked to be having trouble continuing for a moment, and Darcy caught her breath.

'But all this is still supposition. Can you not see that I *had* to take my brother's word over yours? It would not have gone down well with my family if they'd discovered he was lying. Our good reputation is the cornerstone of our rule and it would have near destroyed them. Remember I saw you both with my own eyes, kissing passionately. What else could I think other than you'd discovered you preferred him to me?'

'How can you even *suggest* such a thing? You ask me what it would have done to your family if they'd learned that Xavier wasn't the blue-eyed boy they thought he was…that he'd lied to protect himself and implicated me…but what about the cost *I* paid for being gullible enough to believe that you loved me, Zafir?'

He definitely flushed a little beneath his smooth tanned skin. 'I know it may not seem to you that I value the truth right now, Darcy, but I hope to change that opinion. If it is proved that I have indeed wronged you, then I give you my word that I will do everything I can to put things right… no matter what the personal cost.'

'And you will tell your family the real story? That I was having a relationship with you? That you were confident up until that incident that I would never cheat on you? I told you from the start that I wouldn't consider being intimate with you if my feelings weren't strong. Is it likely I'd go after your *brother*? Anyway, it was cruel of him to not only ensure I lost my job, but to paint such a horrible picture of me…a picture that made it look like I had no morals at all.'

Zafir's lips tightened and his expression was pained. 'I very much regret it if he did that. I will talk to him again about what happened and remind him of what he told me at the time. Then I will give him the chance to think over the accusations he made and be absolutely sure he's telling me the truth. Thankfully he is married now, and appears to be happy. I only pray his good fortune will help guide him to do what is right.'

'And if it doesn't?'

'Then it will be up to me to decide what to do.'

Now Zafir not only looked pained, but weary too.

Darcy had a sudden insight into what a burden it must be to be the head of such a family as his, no matter how admired or influential they were. He had to utilise his wisdom in dealing with many differing personalities, glean what was truly going on in their disputes and act accordingly. And it didn't prevent the individual members of that family from acting purely out of self-interest if they so chose.

She'd discovered long ago that not everyone had a conscience telling them to do what was right...

'By the way, can I verify that you don't have a relationship with anyone right now?'

His examining glance honed in on her like a searchlight.

'I thought I told you that before? No, I don't.'

'That will make things a lot easier.'

'What do you mean? Aren't you engaged? Or did you forget?'

'As far as that's concerned, I will tell you my plans when I have the results of the test. But be assured I will do what is right.'

Darcy chewed down on her lip. 'Right by *whom*, exactly?'

'That's enough.' He couldn't hide his mounting irritation. 'I will talk to you later, when I hear from the clinic. Right now I need to spend some time alone, and that being the case I think it's time I left. Ring me if you need anything, but your top priority should be to rest and recover.'

Just like that he was gone.

The sound of the door closing was like the sound of a portcullis slamming down on her heart. Did he still harbour the belief that she was lying? His brother had sounded so convincing that day—using every trick in the book to make Zafir believe he was sincere, mercilessly using their family relationship to make him doubt his own judgement.

Leaning back against the couch cushions, Darcy shut her eyes tight and tried to jettison the memory of that terrible day from her mind. She'd felt so alone…alone and worthless. If that was the result of her lover not standing up for her, choosing to believe his brother's version of events over hers, then she'd sooner stay single for the rest of her life than risk a similar demoralising situation. But she couldn't stem her deep regret that she and Zafir hadn't been able to put things right and save themselves the unnecessary heartache that had followed...

When the phone rang that evening, just after ten, Zafir all but jumped to snatch up the receiver and answer it. Anyone who had seen him just then would hardly have described him as being cool, calm and collected.

Having abandoned his usual formal attire for a more casual black tee shirt and jeans, he'd been lying on the couch, trying to give his restless attention to a book on the history of the pharaohs and knowing it was utterly pointless. All he'd been able to think about—all he'd *wanted* to think about—was Darcy and the golden-haired child who might turn out to be *his*...

'Am I speaking to His Highness Sheikh Zafir

el-Kalil?' enquired a very circumspect English voice.

'That is correct.'

'Well, sir, I am contacting you about the paternity test you had at the clinic this morning. I now have the results for you.'

'Well?' Zafir snapped, feeling sweat break out on his brow and his heart clamouring even as he unflinchingly infused his tone with authority.

'The test proves that the DNA of the child matches yours, Your Highness. You are indeed the male parent of Master Sami Carrick.'

'Allah Be Praised! The boy is mine!'

Instantly possessive, he had no reservations in displaying his joy and gratification at the news.

I have a son...I have a son...

His heart had never hammered so hard. But he was already making plans as to what he should do first. As well as being portentous, the knowledge that he was a parent was the most incredible thing that had ever happened to him. But there was also a less than desirable aspect to the news. It brought home to him the fact that in effect he had mercilessly abandoned the mother of his child when she'd undoubtedly needed him the most.

That thought alone was like a sharpened scimitar slicing through his gut, and the impact on him was beyond estimation…

'Is there anything else I can do for you, sir?' the clinician enquired.

Staring round at the lavish but tasteful furniture in the elegant room that befitted his status, Zafir couldn't think very much beyond the incredible revelation he'd just heard.

Dazedly he shook his head. 'No. There is nothing else.'

'In that case I'll put the information in an envelope and have it despatched to you by courier just as soon as I can.'

'Tonight would be good.'

'I will aim to do just that, Your Highness.'

The Sheikh's sleek car drew up in front of her house and stopped. The property next door, along with several others in the sedate little cul-desac, didn't suggest much activity—either inside or out. Many of the lights were already extinguished—probably due to it being Sunday and tomorrow the start of the working week.

Its leather-coated driver didn't get out for a full five minutes. His Highness the Sheikh was thinking hard.

He was wondering about the best approach to achieve the result he needed without any argument. If he'd been back in Zachariah there was no question he would have achieved it without dissent. But his royal status hardly held much sway with Darcy, he knew. She was an independent woman, as well as a British citizen, and given that she had given birth in this country she would have certain inalienable rights that he couldn't ignore.

Breathing out a frustrated curse, he pushed back his hair. Tonight he'd deliberately elected to leave Rashid back at the house and drive himself because he needed some privacy. His freedom hadn't been gained without a few strong words from the bodyguard, though, and the assurance that if anything untoward happened he wouldn't be blamed.

At last, deciding to go with his instincts rather than waste any more time devising a plan, Zafir left the vehicle, strode up the pathway and rang the doorbell.

He was very glad that it chimed softly. It was late. If Darcy had gone to bed, he hoped she was still resting on the couch rather than having made the attempt to go upstairs to the bedroom. At least then she wouldn't have to struggle too far to get to the door.

Wearing lilac-coloured pyjamas and a matching robe, the woman who dominated his thoughts above all others opened the door. The blue eyes that were usually so brilliant were visibly drowsy, and her corn-coloured hair curled in mussed gold coils around her shoulders. She was leaning on a single crutch in order to balance and not put her weight down on her injured ankle.

Before he uttered a word, Zafir scooped her up

into his arms and kicked the door shut with the heel of his boot. Still not speaking, he headed straight for the living room. By the dimmed glow of a single lamp he saw that the couch was covered with a rumpled duvet, and the coffee table held a half-eaten sandwich on a plate and what looked to be a congealed mug of tea.

His brow crumpled. 'Was this all you had for your supper?'

'Hello to you too, Your Highness... Didn't you have anything better to do tonight other than to come here, examine my food and annoy me?'

'You would try the patience of a saint, Darcy.'

His tone exasperated, he set her down as carefully as his temper would allow on the couch. Not only would the woman try the patience of a saint, but the feeling of her curvaceous body in his arms and the naturally seductive heat she exuded was apt to make him lose all desire for conversation instantly and want to communicate in a way that would leave her in no doubt as to his feelings.

Did a man ever forget the one woman who had made his breath quicken and his blood surge the moment he had laid eyes on her?

'Presumably you've had the results from the clinic?' she murmured.

'Yes, I have.' Crossing to a plain cream arm-chair, Zafir flicked open the single button on his jacket and settled back in the chair. 'It's just as you said all along...I am Sami's father.'

Bringing her knees up to her chest, Darcy wrapped her arms round them and sighed softly. 'Now you know for sure I wasn't lying.'

The look she gave him was hardly accusing. But it was so nakedly direct that it was like an arrow aimed straight at his heart—an arrow that once it had hit its target broke and embedded its shards in his chest. That soulful, wounded glance would be with him for ever.

Once again, an excoriating sorrow filled him. He had abandoned her. And not just her, but the boy he now knew was his legitimate son and heir...

CHAPTER SIX

LEANING FORWARD IN his seat, Zafir rested his hands on his knees. 'In light of this revelation, you do realise that your life and Sami's will have to undergo some quite radical changes?'

'What do you mean? Are you going to take me to court and sue for custody? Because if you do—if you *dare* even try—I'll...'

'You'll *what*, Darcy?'

Already knowing he would have a fight on his hands if he made any kind of claim on the boy, Zafir also knew that when it came down to it *he'd* have the upper hand. Because of his wealth and status he'd have access to some of the best legal minds in the world to represent him in any dispute. Yet separating the child from his mother had never been a consideration. Seeing Darcy again, and discovering that in spite of the disturbing events that had parted them he was still powerfully attracted to her, had put him in the most agonising quandary. Even more so because during the years they'd been apart she had given birth to his son.

Like a deflated balloon, she sank back against the cushions. She carefully straightened her legs, and he saw her wince as though in pain.

'Don't make me descend into fighting you, Zafir. Don't you think I've been through enough? I can understand that you'll want to get to know Sami, and I'll tell him that you're his father, but what I *won't* do is to let you dictate where he should live or how he's raised. His happiness means everything to me, and despite what you and your family might think of me I *know* I'm a good mother.'

In the edgy silence that followed Zafir fought the strongest urge to go to her and take her in his arms. She seemed particularly fragile tonight, as if the momentous events of the past few days had finally sunk in and shaken her defences. But he decided not to risk worsening their already tense relationship by wading in and making demands straight away. Instead he would try and use tact and diplomacy, and slowly help her come to see that his intention was to help *improve* their lives, not make them harder.

'I don't doubt that you're a good mother. And I can already see how much Sami means to you. You do not have to prove anything to me on that score. And as for my family—they will go along with whatever I decide. Given that I will be informing them I now have a son, there will be much cause for celebration. In fact the whole kingdom will be celebrating.'

'What about your engagement? Do you think your fiancée will be joining in the celebrations?'

It was hard to keep the jealousy from her tone. How on earth was she going to have future dealings with him and pretend that she was well and truly *over* him? Even though she didn't want to admit it, her emotions around him were still raw,

and liable to splinter and shatter if he expected
her feelings to have deadened in the time they'd
been apart. Had *his*?

But his next words truly astonished her.

'I have already decided to bring the engagement to an end. In any case, like I told you, it
was never a love match. Farrida will be gener-
ously compensated for any disappointment she
may have, but she knows how important it is for
me to have an heir. You need not give the matter
a second thought.'

'Do you really believe that, Zafir?' Darcy's
blue eyes flashed. 'As far as your people are concerned, I'm a woman who's not to be trusted,
remember? The woman you fired because you
thought I was cheating on you with your brother.
Do you think they'll accept me and my son after
such a story? It must have done the rounds by
now. I don't doubt they'll think you've lost your
mind to break off your engagement and let me
back into your life.'

'If anyone expresses any doubt whatsoever in

my decisions about my personal life then I will make sure to put them right when I return. But in the meantime it won't help our situation if you and I continue to bring up past disappointments and use them as weapons to cut each other down. Do you honestly think it will help Sami learn to accept me as his father if he sees me as some kind of bully who just tells his mother what to do and seems not to care about her feelings?'

'I don't want him to think that…of course I don't. But the truth is I have no idea *what* you feel about me. Going on past experience, I would say that you cared more about everyone else's feelings than mine.'

'Then you would be wrong.'

'You think? Then why didn't you believe me when I told you I wasn't involved with Xavier? That he had in fact been harassing me?'

Zafir owned to feeling more than just a little uneasy. His brother's reputation hadn't been the only thing called into question. He recalled that at the time leading up to the day when he'd found

Darcy compromised there had been rumours of secret assignations between the pair flying round the office, and they had been substantiated by one of the senior secretaries.

Jane Maddox had been a thirty-something singleton who'd liked to take some of the younger secretaries under her wing. But now Zafir remembered that she'd had a soft spot for his brother, and a tendency to be jealous of any woman younger or prettier than her who might have a chance with him. Being quite a plain woman herself, she'd been particularly jealous of Darcy's beauty. Had she sought to ingratiate herself with Xavier by supporting the lie that the blonde had come on to him?

Many times over the years Zafir had wondered painfully if he'd rashly jumped to the wrong conclusions. If he had, he now knew that it had cost him dear.

'We've been over this. You *know* why,' he answered passionately. 'What was I *supposed* to think when I saw you wrapped in his arms that day? Have you *any* idea what that did to me? It made me go a little crazy. I was jealous, hurt, and mad as hell. There was no time to think rationally about anything.'

'And the relationship we'd had wasn't strong enough for you to trust me?'

'I didn't say that. It's *because* I trusted you implicitly that I was devastated by what looked to be your betrayal.'

'Maybe you should have looked into things a little deeper rather than just accepting what you saw on the surface as being the truth?'

Darcy hunched her shoulders and the pain in her eyes was a fresh wound that ate into his soul.

Breathing out again slowly, she went on, 'I know it's not easy for either of us to forget the past and put it behind us, to forgive and forget and move on. But I too was devastated when you wouldn't listen to the truth. Back then I thought I knew who you were, and there were so many things about you that I admired—particularly your loyalty to family and friends and the way you always tried to help people in need. I thought you were pretty special—and not just because you came from royalty. I didn't care about that. It was the *person* I was interested in, not the trappings. When I first met you I thought you were charming, kind and considerate—unlike any other man I'd met before. I allowed myself to be *seduced* by that man. In short, I grew to trust you, Zafir, and I thought you felt the same way about me. However, I've long since learned that I made the most colossal mistake.'

She was twisting her hands together, and her candid gaze was sorrowful.

The desolate words dried his mouth and made his heart beat too fast for him to think straight. Suddenly the impulse to try and change her mind about him, to make her remember the man she'd once fallen in love with, was overwhelming. It was like a forceful current that threatened to drown him if he didn't act to save himself.

So he went to her, and with gentle but firm hands lifted her up onto her feet. For a long moment he stared into the incandescent blue eyes that usually sparkled like crystal. But tonight… tonight he saw they were bathed in tears…

Just before his lips touched hers, he murmured huskily, 'You didn't make a mistake, *habibi*… perhaps it just wasn't the right time for us?'

Then his mouth slowly and deliberately took hers as his hands held her steady and his senses were suffused by the intoxicating delight that only she could bring. How had he lived so long without it? Zafir longed to touch her body again as he used to, to explore those incredible curves without restraint, and he was frustrated that he couldn't because they weren't alone in the house.

But as the pleasure built inexorably inside him Darcy moaned low in her throat and began to drive her fingers through his hair. There was a hint of wildness, almost of *desperation* in her touch, and he remembered how he'd loved that about her—the way she didn't try to constrain her feelings when they were being intimate. It told him just what he needed to know…that she'd missed the fire and passion they'd once ignited in each other as much as he had, and couldn't help but set a match to it again.

Now the sublime taste of her lips and her silken tongue were arousing Zafir almost to the point of pain. Because the sensations were so intense it was hard to resist her. Hard to not want more, *much* more than just this tempting embrace. But, regrettably, he knew he was going to have to bring their heated exchange to an end. Leave it any longer and it would be near impossible to turn back.

Garnering his resolve, he reluctantly tore his mouth away. Staring back at her, he knew he was breathing hard. Her face was as flushed and pretty as a Millais portrait and once again her blue eyes sparkled like sunlit pools.

'Regrettably, this is not the time or the place for this,' he said 'Your mother and our son are sleeping upstairs and you need to rest that ankle. Sit down...I have something else to say to you before I go.'

Without protest, Darcy let him help her. But when he dropped down beside her on the crumpled duvet he sensed her wariness had returned.

'One of the things I intend to do before I take you home to meet my family is to marry you.' His emotions were taut as a high-wire as he said this, but he forced them back and continued, 'It is a necessary formality so that Sami can take my name and legally have my protection. When we get back to Zachariah we will do things properly and have an official ceremony.'

A doubtful frown crinkled her silkily smooth brow. 'Did I hear you right? Was that meant to be some kind of proposal?'

Zafir's lips twisted wryly. 'I admit it was hardly romantic. But sometimes necessity has to come first. Then later…with time and desire…a man can make up for the deficit and display his true affection.'

'Is that one of your country's philosophies?'

Making his hand into a light fist, he stroked down her delectably soft cheek with his knuckles. Her skin had the same exquisite texture as an infant's.

Tipping up her chin he answered, 'No. I am just expressing that I do not want you to feel short-changed in any way. That I am mindful of what a new bride might understandably expect from her husband.'

Drawing back, Darcy shakily touched her palm to her hair. 'How can I feel short-changed when a proposal is the last—the very *last* thing I want from you?'

'Foolishly, I did not consider the possibility that I'd left you pregnant when we parted, and I confess to being ashamed about that. And know this: it will always haunt me that I did not, because you had to raise our son on your own. I want to make amends. When I learned about him, did you never consider that I might want to meet my responsibilities and marry you?'

'There was a time when I wanted nothing *more* than to be your wife, Zafir. But I don't want to marry you just because you feel you should assume your parental responsibilities. We've been apart for a long time, and many things have changed.'

'That sounds suspiciously like you might want to marry someone else...' After the stratospheric highs of just a moment ago, when he'd kissed her, he came crashing back down to earth—not unlike a brick or a stone that had been dropped from a great height.

'Of course I don't. I'm not even seeing anyone.'

'Then why create obstacles that aren't there?' Zafir knew his eyes must be radiating his confusion and, to be frank, his growing impatience.

'The fact that neither of us trusts each other is a pretty big obstacle, wouldn't you say? It's not something that's easily going to be overcome by a hasty marriage.'

'I have already told you that time and desire will help pave the way to true affection between us. But, more importantly, we need to show our joint commitment to our son. As far as I'm concerned, the sooner we marry the better. I'm not going to be relegated to becoming a part-time father, as seems to be the trend these days in the West, just to suit *you*. The boy is my son and heir and you should not forget that.'

Getting to his feet, he turned round to view her.

'I'm going to leave you now, so you can get some sleep. But tomorrow we will meet for lunch and start the process of putting some plans into place. I'll send a car for you at one o'clock.'

With a glance that he'd resolved would keep a guard on his innermost feelings, Zafir walked to the door and left her alone.

On her return from doing the school run with Sami, Patricia Carrick took off her raincoat and, as was her habit, meticulously hung it on the coat stand. Then she went into the living room to find Darcy.

She wasn't at all surprised to find that her daughter had vacated the sofa, where she'd spent the past couple of nights, but was more than a little annoyed that she had done so. She was supposed to be resting that ankle. But even as a child Darcy hadn't taken to being told what to do, even if it had been for her benefit. In truth, the only person whose advice she had ever really listened to was her father...

Having heard the front door slam shut, Darcy called out, 'I'm in the kitchen, Mum.'

In Patricia's absence she'd washed and dressed and, using her walking cane, had carefully limped into the kitchen to put the kettle on.

'Cup of tea?' she offered.

Standing in the doorway, her mother folded her arms and shook her head in disapproval. 'Do you really think it's a good idea to be pouring out a kettle of hot water in your condition?'

'I've made English Breakfast. I know it's your favourite.'

'Never mind that—did you hear what I said?'

Leaning against the worktop, the younger woman sighed and pushed back the golden tresses that were still spread about her shoulders because she hadn't tied it back yet.

'Yes, I did. You're worried about me pouring hot water from the kettle when I'm on my own having had an accident. For goodness' sake, I'm not a child. I *know* I have to be careful. If I was on my own and didn't have you around to help I'd have to manage.'

'Which brings me to the next thing I want to talk to you about… I want you to tell me the truth about your relationship with the Sheikh. That bank you used to work for in the city…didn't the owners come from a little-known country in the Middle East?'

Feeling discomfited that her mother should mention that right now, Darcy attempted a non-committal shrug. But, having never revealed the identity of her son's father in case of possibly compromising him, she now feared the older woman was fast closing in on the truth.

'What's that got to do with anything?'

'There's something that went on between the two of you in the past, isn't there? I could sense it as soon as I met him. Why on earth would someone as important as he is bring my daughter home from the hospital if he didn't have some kind of vested interest?'

'I worked for him once…that's all.'

'Give me *some* credit, love.' Her mother crossed the floor to draw Darcy's hand into hers. 'Do you think I'm too old to remember what sexual chemistry is like? The air fairly crackles when the two of you are together.'

She was cornered as surely as a fox in a trap…

Chewing down on her lip, Darcy knew she could no longer hide the truth. Even though she'd been even more driven to find Zafir and tell him about Sami when she'd learned he was engaged, she'd lived with the secret for so long without telling anybody that it was going to be hard on her to give up her anonymity. She had never sought fame or fortune, and now it seemed she was going to achieve both…

Last night Zafir had sworn that he was going to marry her, also that they were going to return to his country so he could proclaim Sami his son and heir. An ordinary, simple life would no longer be hers.

There would be no more having to make ends meet on just her own money and her mother's small wage, no more struggling to pay the bills. Whilst some might say that was a *good* thing, she wondered how she could possibly make a marriage work with someone who'd let her down as devastatingly as Zafir had done. Not only that, but with someone who had abandoned her without even giving her a chance to air *her* side of the story.

'Presumably you have told him that Sami is his son?'

'Yes…I've told him.'

'So what does he aim to do about it? I imagine that because he is who he is, his code of honour will be strong…that he will want to do what's right for you and his son?'

Turning away, Darcy reached for the canary-yellow teapot she'd left on the worktop and began to fill two matching mugs. She knew her mother was impatient for her answer but she deliberately didn't hurry to give it.

'Can you put the mugs on a tray and carry it into the living room for me?'

Patricia, her still slim figure attired smartly in a fitted navy skirt and an unfussy white blouse, was exasperated. 'Answer my question… What does the Sheikh intend to do about it?'

Unable to disguise her uncertainty, Darcy sucked in a breath and said quietly, 'He told me that he intends to marry me and make Sami his heir.'

'I knew he was an honourable man the moment I set eyes on him. Now, let's go and have that cup of tea, shall we?'

Much later on that night—in fact in the early hours of the morning—Zafir let the telephone receiver clatter noisily back onto its rest and scraped his hands wearily through his hair.

Making his way into the kitchen, he poured another drink from the coffee pot that his housekeeper always made sure to keep replenished, and uncharacteristically added a couple of sugars. He was in dire need of a caffeine and sugar hit after his testing exchange with Farrida.

As he had guessed, she hadn't taken the news of his cancelling their engagement quietly. She'd expressed the gamut of emotions—from noisy tears and pleas for him to see sense to accusations of him being hypnotised by this woman, who must clearly be holding him to ransom because she'd borne his child.

In the end Zafir had had to exert his authority and tell her once and for all that their engagement was at an end and that he fully intended to marry his child's mother. That Farrida should learn to accept the fact and that her stepping down from their arrangement would be amply compensated. She would retain her lauded reputation as one of the country's most beautiful and accomplished women and be free to marry another distinguished man of her choice.

A short while after finishing his call, the relief

he felt at jumping that particularly testing hurdle was off the scale. It meant that he was now entirely free to marry Darcy without anything standing in his way—because more and more it was dawning on him that she was the one woman in the world he'd always known he was meant to be with.

Sitting in the lobby of one of London's most exclusive hotels, Zafir looked every inch a royal prince. Attired in his traditional dark robes and long leather boots, with his unbound ebony hair gleaming whenever it caught the light, he cut an impressive figure.

Whilst he didn't particularly *want* to announce his status to all and sundry, he saw no reason to hide it. And yet his nature was complex. His father had always said he was a contradiction. One minute he enjoyed the preferential treatment accorded to him by his status, and the next he almost wanted to deny it and disappear into the shadows.

Now, waiting for Rashid to arrive with Darcy, he couldn't help but feel on tenterhooks. When he'd told her that he intended for them to marry and then officially announce Sami as his heir she had seemed anything *but* pleased. That disturbed him. Could she not see at the very least that there were untold benefits for her in becoming his wife? For one thing she wouldn't have to struggle any more, and both she and their son would be supported, cherished and adored by his people for the rest of their lives, not wanting for anything.

But there was one fear in this rosy vision of their future together that Zafir could not easily dissipate. And that was that Darcy would never find it in her heart to forgive him for choosing to believe his brother over her…

'Ms Carrick is here, Your Highness.'

Suddenly Rashid was there in front of him, his eye-catching companion supported by her walking aids beside him.

'Darcy,' he acknowledged, not hesitating to

touch his lips to the side of her cheek. The feeling of her smooth skin and the bewitching imprint of her lovely perfume would stay with him long after she'd gone from him, he mused. 'It is good to see you.'

'You too,' she murmured.

Addressing his guard, Zafir questioned, 'You had a good journey, I trust?'

'Yes, Your Highness. We did not have any problems.'

'Good.'

As Zafir glanced around him he wasn't surprised to note that many of the hotel's visitors and residents gathered in the glamorous lobby were keenly observing their little group. And they were mostly paying attention to Darcy, he saw. Not that he could blame them. Her glorious sunny hair was caught up on top of her head in a very feminine topknot, her make-up was classy and understated, and she was wearing a long jacquard patterned dress with a cinched waistband and a black velvet coat open at the front.

Her beauty was *beyond* stunning. Was it any wonder he was so proud and pleased at the mere sight of her?

Making a quick scan of her flushed features, he immediately checked to see if she wouldn't be better off in the wheelchair. Knowing how stubborn she could be, he didn't want her to risk making her injury worse by insisting on standing when she needn't.

'How are you feeling today?'

'Much better after a decent night's sleep, I'm pleased to say.'

'You are still occupying the downstairs sofa?'

Colouring, she glanced briefly across her shoulder. In case anyone was listening, Zafir thought.

'I hope to change that arrangement tonight and go back to my bed.'

'You think you can manage the stairs?'

'I won't always have you around to carry me, so I had better get used to trying to manage… *Your Highness*.'

She had responded giving him a look that told

him she'd crawl if she had to, rather than accept any more help from him. Whilst he was amused, he was also irritated that she seemed not to remember his assertion last night, when he'd unequivocally told her that he intended to marry her.

'Anyway...we need to get on with our business. I've arranged for us to have some coffee in my suite so we might talk in private. Rashid, you may accompany us and do the usual checks.'

'Of course, Highness.'

Gesturing that Darcy should precede him, Zafir waited until she was ready and confidently in control of her crutches, then led her towards the elevator.

CHAPTER SEVEN

OF COURSE DARCY had experienced the sensation of having butterflies in the tummy before, but never butterflies that felt as if they were *drunk*. But that was just what it felt like as she travelled up to the topmost floor in the elevator with Zafir and his bodyguard.

Their meeting was going to take place in his private suite, he told her. It was a facility he used when he worked late at the bank or needed a private meeting. It would be the first time they'd been properly alone together since contact had been renewed. Naturally she was concerned about how things would go. As far as his desire for marriage went, would he insist on a wedding? Or would he be more reasonable and agree to some kind of compromise? Whilst she didn't doubt that he would be a good father, she was far from certain that he would make an equally good husband…

'Here we are.'

Her striking companion's enigmatic gaze surveyed her thoughtfully as, in keeping with royal protocol, he waited for Rashid to open the door to the suite. He gave her no clue as to what he might be thinking.

The bodyguard went in first to make a quick and efficient reconnaissance. It was another reminder of Zafir's importance that his security was paramount. But when the inspection was over he clearly didn't expect his guard to linger. Instead Zafir instructed him to go and get some lunch and said that he would contact him when they were ready to leave.

'Thank you, Your Highness.' Rashid included Darcy in a respectful, yet cordial little bow and once again she sensed herself warming to the man.

'Darcy?'

With a flourish, Zafir indicated that she should go in before him, and he waited patiently as she complied. The wildly fluttering butterflies in her belly didn't grow any calmer as they entered the suite's sumptuous high-ceilinged sitting room. There were three other doors leading off the area, she saw, and she assumed these must lead to the bedroom and bathroom and perhaps a study? And, if this first room was any indication, presumably they would all reflect the same high level of comfort and good taste.

Furnished with gold-coloured sofas, matching armchairs, stunning framed art that had to be the real thing, and a beautiful Murano glass chandelier, the sitting room was exquisite. On the polished cedarwood surface of an elegant chiffonier was positioned an elegant crystal vase filled with an abundance of scented cream roses. Their perfume all but drenched the air.

Silently acknowledging the congeniality of her surroundings, Darcy consciously steadied her breath to take it all in. Yet what dominated her thoughts above everything else was the fact that she was here *alone* with Zafir.

Owning to feeling nervous, she distracted herself by glancing at the view outside the windows. The soundproof glass rendered the noise of the busy traffic muted and agreeable, and through it she glimpsed the endless green lawns of Hyde Park and the waters of the Serpentine, glinting in the afternoon sunshine. It was clear to her that the guests who occupied the hotel were from a highly privileged world of money and class. Such a view was not open to everyone.

The luxurious ambience inside and out was second to none—this exquisite accommodation was accessed predominantly by the rich and famous. It was already plain that no stone had been left unturned in providing everything a guest might want. And that included a dedicated staff, ready and willing to do their bidding at the drop of a hat.

It was a taste of the elite lifestyle she was contemplating marrying into, Darcy realised, and for a dizzying moment her anxiety increased. How would she adapt to such privileged circumstances if she became Zafir's wife?

Financially, the past few years had been un-questionably hard, and she often didn't sleep at night because she was worrying about how she was going to meet her bills. To have that worry taken away in practically one fell swoop was tan-tamount to a genie suddenly appearing and grant-ing her her most longed-for wish.

Yet she already knew that having money didn't solve everything. For instance it couldn't ease the devastating emotion that followed the death of a loved one…or the catastrophic end of a re-lationship with a lover who had become your sun, moon and stars…both of which she'd expe-rienced personally.

One thing was eminently clear—some proper time for reflection was needed before she made any firm decisions.

Moving away from her companion with the help of her walking aids, she gingerly made her way over to an armchair. Deliberately avoiding the inviting gold-coloured sofas, because the sinful sumptuousness they presented looked as if it might swallow her whole if she sat in one, Darcy got comfortable in the single chair.

There was always a chance that Zafir might decide to join her if she chose the sofa. Right then such a possibility should be avoided at all costs, she decided, because every time he came near her it was like being drugged or put under a spell. The dangerous attraction she'd once had for him had not, it seemed, diminished. In fact it was just as raw and magnetic as it had ever been…

'I've arranged for us to have some coffee and sandwiches,' he announced. 'They should be here soon. Ah…'

There was a sudden knock at the door just as he was speaking, and when he opened it an immaculately attired butler entered carrying a silver tray. At Zafir's behest he proceeded to lay out the tray's contents elegantly on the room's pristine

Burr wood coffee table, and in doing so turned the action into a near art form.

Cordially thanked and tipped, he discreetly left.

Dropping down onto a sofa, her companion remarked, 'I know I suggested lunch, but I've changed my mind. I've decided we should go out for dinner tonight instead. I also think we might take Sami with us.'

Coming out of the blue like that, the suggestion took her aback, and Darcy had immediate reservations. Stroking her hand across her knee under the warm jacquard dress, she replied, 'That wouldn't be a good idea. He's got school tomorrow, and he'll be cranky and tired if he stays up late.'

His lips pursed for a moment, and she saw a muscle flinch at the side of his carved bronzed cheekbone. She didn't suppose he was denied anything very often.

'What can I do but bow to your greater experience as a parent?' he remarked stiffly. 'But, just the same, I won't *always* be so willing to exclude our son from our engagements. He will have to get accustomed to a whole new way of life when we get to Zachariah, and you will soon learn that we do not keep the same hours as you do here. We often eat late.'

'If that's the case, what about his schooling?'

He stared at her as though the question was inconsequential. 'He will, of course, be privately tutored.'

'I take it by that comment you've already assumed we're going back with you?'

There was a flash of gilded flame in his eyes. 'I am fast growing tired of your stubborn resistance. It was my honest intention to be more amenable to your desires, Darcy, but I find I am running out of patience. Once and for all—we are going to be married and we will return home to my country as soon as possible. My plan is that we will spend three months of the year there and divide the rest of our time between London and the States…taking time out in which to have our vacations. Now, let's have some coffee—after which I have some papers for you to sign. Then we will get down to discussing arrangements.'

'What are the papers?'

'One of them is your agreement to marry me. The other is documentation concerning your personal details. You have brought your passport and birth certificate for verification, as I asked?'

Shifting a little in her seat, Darcy's first instinct was to counter this statement with a stubborn reply that would let him know she still had her doubts about the matter, but something told her it wouldn't make any difference…not when he had already firmly decided on what was going to happen.

She would need some time to work out how best to fight her corner, always keeping firmly in mind the needs of her son. They were paramount.

Through tight lips, she answered, 'Yes, I have.' Removing the suede cross-body bag she was wearing, she laid it down on the couch. 'But I'm still not sure that marrying you is the right thing to do. Have you talked to Farrida yet about calling off your engagement?'

'I have. The arrangement is no more, so there is no need for you to worry.'

'And she accepted your change of mind? I imagine that was pretty hard for her to hear.'

'In my country arranged marriages for dynastic purposes are quite usual. They are not complicated by feelings. Farrida accepted the change in my plans with the good grace of the high-born lady that she is.'

The look he gave Darcy was decidedly cool. It conveyed the fact that his mind was definitely made up so no further discussion about it was necessary.

'I see.'

'We are discussing plans for *our* marriage and our return to my country,' he reminded her. 'There is no question that it is right. My son has been too long without the support of his father and your becoming my wife will mean that you no longer have to live a hand-to-mouth existence, unable to provide all the things he needs, the things that are his right as my heir. I think it's time we had that coffee…don't you?'

'I'd prefer tea, if it's all the same to you.'

'Of course—I should have known by now that you don't conform to anything you don't like, Darcy so I ordered some tea as well.' Deftly arranging the cups and saucers on the table as though he wasn't fazed by the domestic task, he teased her. 'Shall I do the honours and pour?'

'I won't say no.'

His big hand fastened incongruously around the delicate porcelain handle of the teapot, and Zafir's silken black eyes glinted with more than just a little provocation. 'How interesting… Tell me, what *do* you say no to?'

Immediately growing warm, she unconsciously smoothed back a curling lock of flaxen hair that had drifted against her cheekbone. If the man had sought to unsettle her with his dangerously suggestive comment then he had succeeded.

'A girl could die of thirst waiting for you to pour that tea, you know.'

Returning the pot to the table, he got slowly to his feet. His dark robes fell back into position with a graceful fluidity that put her in mind of a gently flowing river.

'Are you really so thirsty that you couldn't wait for a few more minutes for that thirst to be satisfied?' he questioned.

Unable to find her voice right then, Darcy gulped. Her breasts were already hot and heavy with desire, and her tightened nipples were tingling fiercely inside a dress that increasingly made her feel as if she was in a steam room. And yet she was intimately aware that the temperature of her body wasn't anything to do with what she was wearing but *everything* to do with the sinfully handsome man who stood in front of her.

She recalled that he'd once told her that his heritage was an ancient one, much revered by historical scholars. How could anyone doubt the provenance of such ancestry? One only had to glance at Zafir's mesmerising visage to be transported into another world... The proud forehead, the carved cheekbones and flowing black hair... all easily brought to mind a culture that was laden with majesty and mystery.

Even so, the people of his tribe had once trekked through the desert on blisteringly hot days searching for watering holes, had spent long, cold nights under a star-filled sky in temperatures probably as bitter as those in the North Pole. Resilience and faith must have been bred into his ancestors' bones for them to have survived such extremes of climate and still make a good life for themselves and their families.

As though intrigued by her silent musing, Zafir gave her a long, slow smile. It was then that Darcy saw his expression was indisputably *hungry*, and she sensed herself succumbing to the unspoken invitation in his eyes as though caught in a sensual undertow she didn't have a prayer of resisting...

'Rather than pour you a cup of tea, I have another suggestion.'

'Oh?'

'Would you not prefer me to make love to you?'

She gasped. 'You shouldn't say such things to me. You—you *know* you shouldn't.'

'Why not?'

He planted himself mere inches from where she sat, so close that his heat mingled irresistibly with the now familiar seductive scent of agar and drifted down to her.

'Would you rather I pretend to be coy, like an inexperienced schoolboy, rather than be a man who intimately knows what he desires and is not afraid to declare it?'

'Doesn't the kind of desire you're alluding to need to be reciprocated?'

'Are you telling me you don't want me, Darcy?'

She felt suddenly quite faint. The things that his deep bass voice alone could do, never mind his looks… Where on earth was she supposed to go with such a question?

'All I'm saying is that I—I need to be sensible, and you're making it impossible for me.'

'Once…not so very long ago…you were my woman. Now we have a child together. That confirms you are *still* my woman.'

'I am no such thing. And nor am I some chattel to do with exactly as you want just because you think it's some inalienable right you have.'

'Is that really how you view me? As someone who wouldn't even *consider* another person's rights if they happened to conflict with my own? That is a shame. But, that aside, if you're saying that you no longer have any feelings for me other than hatred, then I have to remind you that I am still the father of your son and I fully intend to claim my paternal rights—with or *without* your approval, because my people need an heir.'

Although Darcy's heart was racing, her voice was calm when she replied, 'I don't hate you. I never did—despite what happened. But my child's well-being and future are not up for being bartered with.'

'It is not my intention to barter.'

A maddening smile touched the corner of his lips, as if he already knew he held the trump card.

In response, a wave of exasperation bubbled up inside her and suddenly burst free. 'Look…you had your chance with me once, Zafir, but you threw it away. Yes—threw it away as though it was nothing. My trust was destroyed when you did that. It was smashed into the dust. If you think it can be so easily reinstated by giving in to plain *lust* then I have to tell you in no uncertain terms that it can't.'

The look she saw in his eyes just then mesmerised her. She suddenly knew that he wasn't going to respond as she'd thought.

'My desire for you is not born out of plain *lust*, Darcy. I still have feelings for you, despite any ill-advised actions I may have taken in the past. And now a child—*our* child—has been brought into the equation. That alone changes everything. Can we not make our peace…at least for *his* sake?'

An audible groan escaped her. She sensed the last vestiges of her resistance melt helplessly away, and knew she was fighting a losing battle to stay strong. 'I would do anything for Sami.'

'You may not know it yet, but so would I.'

Knowing he meant it, Darcy felt her aroused senses wanting to dance to a whole different tune from the one she'd intended. Unprotestingly, she succumbed to the compulsion.

As if already aware of her decision, Zafir carefully guided her up onto her feet. His big hands circled her waist, and she was glad it had remained so slender after her pregnancy.

'What else do I have to do to make you know how much I want you?' he asked huskily. 'And not just purely to satisfy my craving for your body. There are many reasons why I desire you. Although it's a long time since we were together like this, the memory has never left me. Did you think it would?'

Warring with the urge to lay her hand against his bronzed cheek, she knew her voice was a tremulous whisper as she said softly, 'You don't play fair, you know... But then...you never did.'

'I think our refreshments can wait.'

Without warning, he lifted her high into his arms against a chest that anyone could see was magnificent. And she could personally attest to the fact that it had muscles like steel and skin as sensuously smooth as satin. The smile he gave her was unashamedly knowing and sexy, and it spoke of things that only lovers had shared.

In the past there had been many times when he'd buckled her knees with such a look. What woman could resist such hot temptation for long? No matter how stoic her vow, she wouldn't be human if she refused him—and Darcy had never forgotten the time she'd spent in his arms. She hadn't been able to resist him then and neither could she do so now.

'We have a lot of time to make up for.'

Zafir headed purposefully towards the bedroom and forced the chic double doors open with the toe of his boot. As soon as they'd entered the room he carried her across to the canopied bed...

Removing his boots, and helping Darcy dispose of her leather flats, Zafir lay down with her on the bed. For long minutes they clung together on top of the counterpane, just staring at each other. The only sound they heard in those timeless few moments was the slow in and out of each other's breath.

But then he lowered his head and started to kiss her.

It was akin to pouring petrol on a fire.

Those initial experimental kisses quickly turned into a conflagration of desire and passion as they eagerly started to rediscover each other. When they stopped for a while, to draw breath, Darcy threaded her fingers through his hair.

'It still feels like silk. What made you decide to grow it?'

Smiling down into her eyes, he chuckled. 'It is a family tradition, I guess. Do you like it?'

She dimpled. 'I do. I like it very much.'

'I will have to tie it back for a while.'

'Why?'

He was already reaching into his tunic to produce the black velvet ribbon he carried should this need arise. Right now Zafir wanted nothing to impede his view of his lover.

'I want to see you…in fact I want to see *all* of you.'

Deftly securing the ribbon around the ponytail he'd fashioned, he never once withdrew his gaze from Darcy.

Like a trained musician who never forgot how to play the notes his very soul was imbued with, he began carefully to peel the clothes from her slim yet curvaceous body. His sense of awed reverence as he did so took his breath away. She was just as beautiful and perfectly formed as he remembered—and her scent and her skin were casting a spell on him that made him fiercely glad to be alive.

During the years they'd been apart he'd often

dreamed of her. And, vivid as those dreams had been, they had more often than not *tortured* him. What good were dreams when they only served to remind him of what he had lost? But even those enticing images of Darcy his mind had so helpfully conjured up couldn't hope to come near to the reality of having her here with him in the flesh.

After giving in to his voracious need to divest her of her clothes, Zafir briefly stood up to draw the sumptuous voile hangings of the canopy around them. The delicate but effective shield immediately helped reduce the daylight that streamed in through the windows and he started to remove his robes.

Just before he leant towards her his hypnotised glance drank in the sight of her perfectly pale rounded breasts and he saw that her delicate pink nipples were already puckering...just as if they waited for his touch. Although he ached to take them into his mouth and suckle he wanted to touch his mouth to hers again first.

His glance holding hers, he savoured her pert, plump lips as though they were an opening to nothing less than the nectar of the gods. And they *were,* he acknowledged as his tongue swept the hot satin interior and feverishly duelled with hers. Each hungry kiss stoked a fire inside him that had never burned so hot with any other woman but *her*, and the near pain in his groin when he didn't immediately take her was testimony to his voracity and need.

Suddenly aware that her hands were pushing against his chest she freed her lips from his.

'Have you *any* idea what you're doing to me?'

'I hope I'm turning you on, angel.'

'You are, Zafir. But there's something I want to tell you—something I should have told you a long time ago.'

His body stilled. 'What is it? What didn't you tell me before, Darcy?'

She knew she was trembling. She was unable to help herself. *Would he believe her?* She had been so eager for him that night, and she had let her feelings dictate her actions, telling herself that everything would be all right.

'The first time we made love at the hotel…on our special night out…do you remember?'

The corners of his lips lifted in a knowing smile. 'Of course I remember. My heart gallops even now at the memory.'

Her throat tightened. 'Well…you didn't seem to mind my lack of experience, which I was sure I couldn't help but show, and I thought perhaps it didn't matter because you didn't mention it… But I was a *virgin*, Zafir. You are the first and only lover I have ever had.'

His face visibly drained of colour. 'If that is true…I *should* have noticed. But you only expressed pleasure, not pain. Did I hurt you that first time?'

She wrapped her hand around his. 'There was initial soreness, but after that everything fell beautifully into place and I just thought it *wonderful*.'

'But why didn't you *tell* me? How can you not know that it is the greatest gift a woman can give to a man?'

'I suppose I feared that it didn't count for much these days if a woman wanted to save herself for…for someone she cared for.' Darcy wouldn't say *loved*. That was one step too far right now, and she'd already risked too much. 'I thought that most men wanted somebody experienced.'

'You're crazy…where did you learn that?'

'Most women I talked to seemed to think of being experienced as an asset. I never went along with that.' She knew she blushed. 'I guess I've always been a bit of a romantic.'

'I'm glad that you are.'

He swept back her hair from her forehead and planted a kiss there. His velvet eyes seemed suddenly to darken with desire.

'Do you still want me?'

'I do…I want you *now*, Zafir.'

'I want you, too.'

'Then don't make me wait any longer.'

* * *

He saw with satisfaction the indubitable hunger in her eyes.

'I won't leave you waiting for long, my angel,' he promised, 'but I need to use protection. I have it here, in the pocket of my robes.'

As he turned to collect the garment he'd left on the bed Darcy stayed his hand. Her smile was unsure and shy again, he saw.

'I'm—I'm on the pill now, so it won't be necessary.'

Zafir's heart thumped hard, in spite of the fact she'd already told him she wasn't seeing anyone else. Now he'd learned that she'd been a virgin when they'd first made love, he hated the thought that she might have had another man in her bed after their split...

'I had to protect myself after—after what happened before,' she explained.

'But you *wanted* Sami? You wanted to have our baby?'

Widening the azure-blue eyes that contained

the mesmerising hues of both sea and sky, she answered, '*Always*. He is everything to me…you *have* to know that.'

'There is no doubt in my mind, *habibi*. I only have to look at the two of you together to be assured.'

Without comment, she wound her slender arms possessively around his neck and pulled him fervently down to her.

Zafir needed no further bidding. Pressing her deep into the bed, he felt his blood pumping hard in anticipation of making her his again. Sliding his hands beneath the tender silk of her bottom, he nonetheless took his time in guiding her slim legs round his middle, so as not to jolt her ankle.

But quickly the molten desire that was building inexorably inside him took command, and he didn't hesitate to ease deep inside her. He thought he might have offered up a prayer of thanks at the moment of contact, but he couldn't be sure. All he knew was that it was an altogether dizzying as well as supremely satisfying experience to be so intimately acquainted with her again.

No other woman could make him feel the way Darcy did. And knowing that she'd had his child after he'd so foolishly and painfully rejected her, discovering she'd been a virgin that first time, made the undoubted bond they'd once forged even more meaningful now...

His glance hungrily sought hers as he raised himself to look down at her. Guided by a force that was as ancient as time itself he started to move more rhythmically inside her, registering with pleasure her softly quivering lips as she moaned low. Claiming them in a hot, hard kiss, he lifted her arms high above her head as he plunged deeper. His action quickly elicited the re-action he'd hoped for. Raising herself up to meet him, her body suddenly contracted.

'Oh, Zafir,' she moaned ardently, her satin-soft thighs gripping him hard.

Glancing down at her, he saw she had tears in her eyes as she irresistibly came apart in his arms...

CHAPTER EIGHT

ZAFIR WAS INDEED a man of contradictions, Darcy thought as she lay wrapped in his arms, her hand idly resting against the curling dark hair on his impressive chest. Not only was he a hot and passionate lover, he was also a touchingly considerate one. Twice he had deliberately delayed the culmination of his own pleasure until she had reached hers, and now after the second time he lay down beside her, gave her a wry smile and teased her.

'Either I'm seriously out of practice or your sexual drought has rendered you insatiable, my love. I am all but worn out.'

'Are you saying that you can't keep up with me?' she responded, at the same time registering with delight that he'd called her his *love*.

'I trust that is a joke?'

Darcy grinned. 'Do you really think I'd have the *nerve*, as a subordinate, to call your sexual prowess into question, Your Highness? I wouldn't dare! I'm sure people have been thrown into dismal dark dungeons for less.'

'You'll pay for that disrespectful remark, you little minx.'

Turning and fastening his hands round her waist, he effortlessly hauled her on top of him with a fierce look. It wasn't even remotely threatening, yet never had he looked more like a warrior than he did right then. His dark hair was still tied behind his head with the black ribbon, and the style drew immediate attention to his iron jaw and hollowed cheekbones as his smouldering dark gaze mercilessly took her prisoner.

Eagerly possessive and desirous, she felt as limp as a rag doll when she gazed back at him. Perhaps he was right. Perhaps she *was* insatiable...at least as far as he was concerned.

'I vow that I will make it my life's work to

keep you pleasured until the end of our days, my Queen,' he taunted her.

'That's all well and good, but I'm hardly a *queen*.'

'Not yet…at least not officially…but you soon will be. In my country I am King, and naturally the woman I marry becomes Queen.'

'If that's intended to reassure me, it *doesn't*. To be frank, it makes me want to run away and hide.'

Zafir's breath momentarily grew still. 'Are you serious? Why would you want to do such a thing?'

'Because I've always lived a fairly quiet life, and now it seems I'm going to be thrust into the limelight.'

'You will grow into the role, my sweet—as those of us born onto this path *have* to. But, remember, I will always be there by your side to help you.'

Overcome by the declaration, Darcy made to move away. But her lover dropped his hands firmly onto her slender thighs and held her fast. Her blood instantly slowed and then pumped sluggishly with the heat of molten lava as it became evident he was already aroused.

'Don't go away. All I want to do is to make you feel good. Have you forgotten how it used to be between us? What finally drove us into bed?'

'I remember. And I don't deny the old attraction between us is still there. But it doesn't mean that we can make things right again so easily.'

'If I have caused you pain at *any* time then I sincerely regret it. But we have a son now, and I want to try and make amends for the wrongs of the past. Can you not see that my intentions are sincere?'

Wanting desperately to believe him, Darcy was still wary of letting down her guard. The proof of the pudding was in the eating. She prayed Zafir's declaration was genuine but, glancing at him right then, she found herself helplessly captured by the sight of his rippling smooth muscles and powerfully built shoulders.

She knew already how hard it was to resist him. Seeing the shamelessly inviting look in his slumberous ebony eyes, she felt her breath catch. It would be oh, so easy to give in to the temptations of the flesh and discount all that had gone before in the hope that, given time, her trust would be repaired. Then again, would she be a fool for giving in so easily and then, a little bit further on down the line, come to regret it?

'You do not answer, and that perturbs me.'

'It's just that good intentions aren't always fulfilled…no matter how strong the desire.'

'I think all this talk is complicating what should be very simple. All we need to ask right now is *do* we desire each other or *don't* we? I know what my answer is.'

Zafir cupped her face and immediately brought her mouth down to his. His hands were large and warm next to her skin, and oddly protective. The kiss quickly became languorous and deep, with Zafir's hot, silken tongue hungrily sweeping the soft satin textures inside her mouth and seductively duelling with hers. A charge of demanding sexual need swept through her.

'Your breasts are like velvet ivory...the touch and the texture of your skin exquisite. Can you remember how it felt when I touched you there?' he whispered against her neck.

Stunning her, he filled his hands and captured her nipples between his fingertips. His lascivious glance unflinching, he shamelessly added some pressure and pinched hard...

She nearly shot through the roof at the dizzying sensation of pain mingled with pleasure. Then he took one nipple into his mouth and suckled. Throwing back her head, Darcy whimpered. Her hair had already been coming adrift from the tortoiseshell clip, and now the golden strands loosened even more.

Zafir's hungrily searching hands began to explore the rest of her...he was running his hands freely over her body. In the meantime her hair brushed against the nipples he had so erotically inflamed and she couldn't suppress a feverish groan. Against the tenderness of her flesh the strands felt more like knives rather than something so innocuous…

'I never *could* get enough of you,' he confessed huskily.

Leaning towards him to fully receive his kiss again, all she could manage in reply was a murmured, 'Mmm…'

In less than a heartbeat, he thrust inside her. He was hard, hot, and everything she could have wished for, and straight away their bodies fell into a sensual rhythm.

Feeling dazed with relief at having this basic but very necessary human need fulfilled, she realised how much she'd missed the carnal satisfaction this man could deliver. She was thrilled by the touch of his mouth against hers, and his avid response told her he felt the same. No matter how much time had passed since they'd first become lovers, it seemed their physical desires remained perfectly in tandem. And with intimacy came the knowledge that she was somehow able to set aside the devastation and heartache she'd endured and focus her attention purely on the present.

It was a welcome revelation. The truth was that all she'd ever wanted from Zafir was his *love*… passionate, devoted and undying. Anything less would just not be good enough.

Darcy had the distinct sense that time had slowed down, and now it was stopping altogether as she was in Zafir's arms. All she was aware of was *him*. One caress flowed into another like a seamless symphony, as though they had never forgotten which note came next. She didn't want his amorous attentions to end. Together they were creating a magical world of their own, where no one could intrude or make demands, and she revelled in the freedom of that.

When the urgency of their lovemaking came to a wholly gratifying end they lay back together on the cool sheets beneath the counterpane. Her satisfying sense of fulfilment thankfully didn't disperse quickly. Instead of feeling almost numb to the idea of experiencing intimacy again, Darcy wondered how she had managed so long *without* it. Yet again the man at her side had awakened feelings in her she'd been sure she'd buried long ago. The notion that they'd been revived and might possibly remain in that state for many years to come couldn't help but tantalise her.

With a sigh, Zafir turned towards her. Lifting his hand, he let his artistic fingers explore her face with fascination. They put her in mind of a master sculptor, so enamoured of his craft that he wanted to imprint the shape and texture of the features he studied on his memory for always.

The very notion that he should want to do such a thing made Darcy's heart race. For such a masculine man his touch was remarkably gentle, and what woman *wouldn't* revel in the carnal feelings it instigated?

But all of a sudden he looked perturbed.

'You tell me there has been no one in your life since me…' He frowned. 'But during all these years have you not missed having a man to hold you and make love to you? Knowing how passionate you are, I cannot believe you have never longed for that.'

In truth, she had forgotten how frank Zafir could be sometimes. Now she recalled how he always cut to the chase rather than beating around the bush.

Her cheeks flaring with heat, she replied, 'Occasionally I've missed not having someone to hold me—yes, of course I have. The single life gets lonely sometimes. But I've not wanted another relationship since I had Sami. I certainly haven't missed the physical side of things so much that I would risk bringing a stranger into my son's life.'

'It pleases me to hear that. Your devotion to our son is commendable. It reaffirms that my decision to marry you is the right one.'

'And you, Zafir?'

Focusing her attention on him so she wouldn't misread his expression, Darcy tucked some drifting tendrils of hair around her ear. In the throes of their lovemaking her disarrayed hair had fallen down past her shoulders.

'Have you had many other women in your life since me?'

She almost held her breath.

'I suppose it is only fair that you should ask me that.'

Reaching behind him, he arranged his pillows behind his back and sat up.

His powerful shoulders tensing, he glanced round at her. 'I don't deny that in my position I have many opportunities to meet beautiful and well-connected women. But that doesn't mean I want to sleep with them all. And if all I wanted was to be with someone suitable who met with the dictates of my family do you not think I would have gone ahead and married Farrida?'

Now she sat up too. Tugging the counterpane a little further to cover her breasts, she drew up her knees. 'It's just that you're a very attractive and virile man, and I can't see you willingly going without—without sexual attention for very long.'

His answer was part grimace and part smile. 'You're right, of course. But it goes against my personal code to be promiscuous, so when I first returned to Zachariah after our relationship ended I took a mistress. We entered into what you might call a business arrangement, in so far as there were no feelings involved. But it wasn't long before we parted. The whole thing felt indescribably empty to me. That was when I resolved to get on with my life and put my energies into running the business.'

Her mouth drying at this latest revelation, Darcy listened intently. But her heart still clamoured painfully at the thought of him being with other women.

She forced herself to ask, 'So, because it felt so empty, you decided it was a better option to marry Farrida? At least you know her family. When did you meet up with her again?'

'We bumped into each other at a function in New York. She reminded me of our families' hopes that we would marry if we hadn't met anyone else by the time we reached thirty.' He shrugged. 'Well, I was thirty-six and she was thirty-five. She'd had a couple of relationships that hadn't worked out and she told me she was getting "broody".'

He flushed a little under his skin at the phrase.

'It was most unlike her. She's never been one for sentiment. Time was running out, she said. And, knowing that I was still single and needed an heir, she thought it the ideal solution that we get together.'

'So you agreed that you would get engaged?'

Zafir's expression was rueful, but frank. 'I did. As I've already indicated, the agreement was a purely pragmatic one.'

'And then *I* turned up again.'

'I can only thank the powers that be that you did…especially when I found out that I already have the heir that I longed for.' He affectionately drew his fingers down her cheekbone.

'But I'm neither suitable nor well-connected, Zafir… What if your family don't approve of us marrying? What if they suggest you make me your mistress instead?'

His hand lowered to cup her chin and his dark eyes were unflinchingly possessive. 'You are most definitely going to be my wife, Darcy… *not* my mistress.'

'And that's really what you want, is it?'

His eyes narrowed. 'Do you honestly need to ask me that? Haven't I already made my feelings more than clear?'

She shrugged a shoulder. 'I'd like to think that everything you've told me is true, but after what happened last time I'm understandably wary.'

'Are you saying that you will never trust me again?'

'No. That's not what I'm saying. But it's going to take me some time.'

'I cannot say I like that…but I understand. So I will ask you again—do you agree to marry me?'

'Yes, I do.' The slight smile she gave him was fleeting. 'Seeing as you *are* my son's father, and that you intend to honour your responsibilities as far as he's concerned, I know it makes sense.'

Zafir's own smile was wry. 'Indeed… But you could also endeavour to look a little happier about the prospect. Our son's life *and* yours are definitely going to change for the better.'

'I'm sure time will tell,' Darcy murmured.

Reaching down to where Zafir had discarded her clothes, she matter-of-factly pulled her dress over her head, balled up her underwear in her hand and wriggled to the end of the bed. Once there, she moved the voile hangings to one side and, testing her ankle, gingerly stood up.

'Where are you going?' he demanded, his tone sounding irritable.

'I'd like to have a bath… It's easier than negotiating a shower.'

'Of course.' His expression visibly relaxed.

'Can you help me to set things up?'

'I will do more than that. I'll accompany you and make sure you have everything you need.

You're going to need my help, getting in and out of the bath.'

Knowing that she wasn't exactly in a position to refuse, she reluctantly nodded. 'You won't have to do this for much longer, you know. When my ankle is better I'll—'

'I know it's your nature to want to be independent, Darcy, but sometimes...'

Joining her, he firmly turned her towards him and she gasped. He was shamelessly naked—hadn't even paused to grab a sheet to wrap around him.

As his warm breath gently fanned her face he smiled. 'Sometimes it doesn't hurt to accept help...yes?'

The next day Zafir went in to his plush office at the bank. Having grabbed some coffee on the way, he sat down at his desk and buzzed Jane Maddox, one of the senior secretaries, to come in. Studying her over the steaming cup as she entered, he straightaway noted that her perfume was a little on the overpowering side.

You could tell a lot about a woman by the perfume she wore, he mused. It certainly didn't make him warm to the brunette, even though he'd never found fault in her work. But, more importantly, today he wanted answers to questions that were long overdue.

'Sit down,' he instructed, indicating the leather chair opposite him at the desk.

'I trust all is well, your Highness?'

Intent on keeping the secretary on edge, he took his time responding. When he did reply, his tone was deliberately aloof. 'That rather depends on your answers to my questions, Ms Maddox.'

Her thin, rather drawn face couldn't hide her disquiet. 'May I know the topic of these questions, sir?'

'You may.'

He bit back the fury that had been simmering inside him since he'd heard that Darcy had tried to contact him many times, to no avail. This woman was in charge of his administration, and if anyone knew what had happened to all Darcy's messages it was her.

He let the woman have the full force of his gaze. 'The topic, Ms Maddox, is Darcy Carrick...'

They were about to be married.

They were having a simple, dignified ceremony at one of London's most famous register offices and their two witnesses were Rashid and Darcy's mother, Patricia, who diligently held their son's hand.

As the male celebrant began to lead them through their vows Zafir had had a sense of everything being quite surreal. He'd been crazy about the woman at his side from the very first moment he'd set eyes on her, and knew that his decision to marry her couldn't be more right. But the fact that they'd originally separated due to what was beginning to look like the most terrible misunderstanding on his part didn't sit well with him.

It didn't sit well at all.

Especially now Jane Maddox had admitted that she'd made the decision not to pass on any messages from Darcy because she hadn't wanted to upset him all over again. In her opinion, she'd done him a favour.

'How dare you make such a judgement on my behalf?' he'd demanded coldly. 'Just who do you think you are?'

Zafir was by no means a violent man, but he didn't know how he hadn't immediately throttled her. Instead, he'd had great satisfaction in telling her to collect her things and leave the building, never to set foot in it again.

With a heartfelt sigh he glanced at Darcy and again was taken aback by her beauty. Not only did she resemble the mythical Aphrodite, goddess of beauty, love and sexual rapture, but she had a beautiful heart too. She hadn't hesitated to raise their son on her own when she'd been abandoned by him and that told him a lot. Now Zafir aimed to make it up to her in whatever way he could.

It grieved him deeply that he'd unknowingly turned his back on her when she'd been pregnant with his child. But how could he even have suspected that was the case? How did a man even *begin* to come to terms with such a thing? He wished that his father still lived. He was the only person who could have helped him with his sage advice…

When the time came for him to repeat his vows he nearly missed his cue because he was so lost in the tumult of his feelings. He'd missed not having intimate relations with Darcy in the days leading up to the wedding, but she'd explained that she needed some time on her own with Sami.

Zafir hadn't been able to argue with her when she'd told him that she wanted to introduce him to the idea of her getting married sensitively, and also to inform both his school and her employers that they would shortly be leaving to start a new life abroad.

In light of that, Zafir had agreed to abstain from any intimacy until they were married. He was already feeling the strain.

He'd worked hard to bring the ceremony forward, but it had still been several days before he'd been able to make it happen. In the interim, he had utilised his time wisely. First of all he had rung his mother, to give her the news. Admittedly she had been upset when he'd broken off his engagement to Farrida, but she had been overjoyed when she'd learned he had a son and heir.

Even though she didn't know the woman who was the mother of his child, she had agreed that it was the right thing to do to marry her. She knew he wouldn't have made such a decision if he didn't care for her. Understandably, she still had a lot of questions, but Zafir assured her that they would all be answered to her satisfaction on his return. He'd also told her that his new family would need some time to adapt to their new situation, and to their royal status, and had asked her not to advertise the fact that he was coming home with them straight away.

They would all need a little privacy for a while…at least until the official wedding took place.

His second phone call had been to his brother. He had told him they needed to have a serious talk, and Xavier had responded with an unusual equanimity in his voice.

'I will very much look forward to that, my brother. I, too, have some important things I need to tell you.'

He had sounded almost *eager* at the prospect, and it had made Zafir wonder at the reason for this new affability.

For today's ceremony Zafir had relinquished his traditional garb for a tailored tuxedo, and Darcy wore a simply cut classic cream suit trimmed with lace that her mother had bought her. He was glad that he hadn't insisted that he buy her a dress, because it seemed important to both women that they'd had their way. Darcy had her golden hair styled in an elegant chignon, with a delicate crystal and seed pearl headband to complete the stunning look.

In Zafir's eyes, she had never looked more like a princess than right at this moment. He was excited at the prospect of introducing his new bride to his people when they had their official wedding in Zachariah, and was already considering making the day a public holiday in honour of the occasion. But, more important to him than that, he could hardly wait to introduce his son and heir.

He was truly looking forward to getting to know his little boy. One day Sami was going to be a ruler they would all be proud of.

CHAPTER NINE

SITTING BESIDE HER son in the plush leather seats of a private jet, Darcy felt like pinching herself to make sure she wasn't dreaming. Once upon a time, when her love for Zafir had been new and fresh, she'd often fantasised about them being together for good. However, in her private moments, before everything had gone so wrong, she'd also known that realistically it wasn't likely to happen.

How could it? He was an important person in the world while she…well, she was a million miles away from inhabiting such an elevated sphere as he did.

It had been more than painful to contemplate a life without him…akin to being flayed alive… And then had come another twist in the tale and fate had given her Sami. Once again, her world had been utterly shaken.

And when she'd finally set eyes on Zafir again, after so long trying to contact him, having plunged from the wall of his house in her urgency to see him, their bittersweet reunion had left her reeling. Even now Darcy was still struggling to come to terms with the way events had transpired. Not least, she thought, contemplating the diamond-encrusted gold wedding band on her finger, the fact that she and her illustrious ex-boss were now married and heading out to his home in Zachariah.

'I like this plane, Mummy. It's cool.'

'What?' Lost in thought, she flushed when she realised that both her son and his father were studying her intently. 'Yes, it is, darling. Aren't we lucky to get to travel like this? Not everyone is so fortunate.'

Falling silent for a moment, the tousle-haired little boy turned his gaze on Zafir. 'Do you really live in the desert?'

Having forgone the traditional robes he usually wore, her husband was wearing dark jeans that emphasised his taut-muscled thighs teamed with an ebony-coloured cashmere sweater. Whatever he wore, the man always looked effortlessly classy. She supposed it must be in the blood.

Leaning forward with a conspiratorial smile, he replied, 'I do, indeed… My family and I have our own kingdom.'

'What's that?' Sami's big brown eyes were on stalks.

'It's our own private country.'

'Are there any dragons there?'

His father chuckled. 'I'm sorry to say we don't have any dragons. The main creatures we have are camels and horses. But nevertheless it is still a magical place, my son.'

The fact that Zafir so often referred to Sami as his son when speaking to him made her insides somersault. The little boy had very quickly taken to the idea that the Sheikh was his father, and she found it touching that he'd accepted him so readily. At least Darcy didn't have any worries on *that* score.

'He has a very creative imagination,' her husband remarked, and his twinkling glance at her made her feel as if she was being massaged with some heavenly warm oil. 'It clearly must come from his mother.'

'Oh, I don't know—I'd say his father is no slouch in that department either.'

'What's a slouch, Mummy?' Sami asked, yawning.

She bit her lip at the amused, knowing gleam in the Arabian's eyes.

That first time they'd made love he'd introduced her to the art like a connoisseur. He had ensured his every touch was exquisite and meaningful on the magical road to her fulfilment, even though he'd been as passionately hungry as she was. He might not have known at the time that she was a virgin, but he'd treated her like one.

He was by no means a selfish lover. Many times that night he'd conveyed by both word *and* deed that it wasn't something he ever took lightly… that it was important to him that his lover was at the very least treated like a princess.

Darcy had never forgotten that night. She couldn't help anticipating that her wedding night would be equally unforgettable…

As though reading her mind, Zafir asked lazily, 'Are you tired? It's been quite a week for you, what with one thing and another. No doubt you must be looking forward to going to bed?'

Knowing the hot colour in her face must easily betray her, she said quickly, 'I'm not tired, but I know who *is*.'

She could already sense the way her son's warm weight was slumping in her arms and she was glad for him. It would make the transition to this new country a little easier for them both if he got some sleep.

They arrived in the balmy temperatures of early evening. The warm air was laden with the exotic and mysterious perfumes of the desert, and anyone who wasn't a local would only have to shut their eyes and breathe it in to know they must be in an ancient landscape—a land where magic and mystery still predominated.

Those attributes were undoubted blessings, in Zafir's eyes. They were equally as powerful as its history, he believed.

On the plane he had given Darcy the news that his mother was sending a royal escort to meet them, and he hoped that she wouldn't feel overwhelmed by a procedure that for him and his family was commonplace. This was one of the privileges she would have to get used to, he'd told her.

But he'd instructed his retainers that their arrival home shouldn't be made known to the public immediately, as his family had some major readjustments to make first. This was a new situation for all of them, and they would all have to learn to adapt.

As Zafir guided Sami down the steps of the plane, then returned to assist his wife, he immediately sensed her anxiety. Although the white stretch limousine that stood waiting on the Tarmac would be impressive by anyone's standards, no doubt it might be daunting to anybody not used to experiencing such an elite way of travelling. It would be further confirmation to Darcy that her life really *had* begun to change for the better.

The chauffeur had already opened the car doors, Zafir saw, and now the dependable Rashid—who'd been sitting at the back of the plane to give him and his family some privacy—dutifully joined him.

'I will see to the luggage, Your Highness.'

'Thank you, Rashid.'

Having undertaken the task, his loyal retainer transported the baggage out of the plane and, with the chauffeur's assistance, deposited them in the boot.

Once inside the vehicle, the small family sat together—that was until Sami asked if he could sit on one of the seats that hugged the sides, in order to look out of the windows. Although tinted on the outside, from the inside everything was seen just as though the panes were clear glass.

'You may sit wherever you want, Sami. I can sit next to you, if you like, then if you have any questions about what you see, you can ask me,' his father told him.

'Will we see some pyramids?'

Zafir's lips curved in amusement. He was already enchanted by his son. 'No. We don't have them in this country. But we do have other spectacular sights to see. This is a land as old as time itself, and its history is remarkable.' As he said this, the great pride in his voice was unmistakable.

As they progressed towards his desert home, very soon leaving the main city behind, Zafir expelled a relieved sigh. In truth, he was glad to be getting away from the rest of humanity for a while—glad to be pulling up the drawbridge and just being with his family. Marrying Darcy and becoming acquainted with his son had made him realise that this was what he had *always* longed for...to have a family of his own.

But it was *Darcy's* presence that preoccupied him the most. After so long apart, he liked to think he was starting to get to know her again. Yet she never failed to surprise him. It was her beauty that had first attracted him, but she was so much more than that. He'd since discovered that she was fiercely loyal to those she loved, was hard-working, funny, and quite often contrary. There would never be a dull moment when they were together and he'd be a fool to take her for granted.

She was extraordinarily intuitive about what to wear too. Today, in deference to meeting his mother, she was wearing a very graceful mocha-coloured maxi-dress with a slim white jacket. Her pretty hair had been fashioned into plaits that she'd styled into a corona and fastened with an elegant gold clip that he'd bought her. She looked young and ravishing—just like a fairytale princess about to enter a palace that might have been created just for her.

'How are you holding up?'

When she turned her shimmering blue gaze towards him his insides rolled over, just as though he'd plunged to the earth from the greatest of heights. He couldn't envisage a time when he would ever tire of looking into their silken depths. She was like an angel who rendered him spellbound.

'I'm fine.'

There was the briefest glimpse of that guarded smile he sometimes saw, and Zafir wondered if she would ever look at him with complete trust in her eyes, as she had done in the early days when they'd first been together. He swallowed hard at the thought that she might not.

'And your ankle…the injury is not bothering you so much today?'

'No. It's definitely on the mend, thank goodness. How about you? How are *you* feeling? I know how important today must be for you.'

Taken aback by her thoughtfulness, he couldn't deny his pleasure and his answering smile was wide and freely given.

'I'm good. Why wouldn't I be, when I am about to introduce my wife and son to my mother for the very first time? I'm as excited at the prospect as I know she is.'

Darcy's first sight of the palace was one she would never forget. From a distance it looked like an ice castle, rising out of the earth, its crystalline perfection so exquisite it was breathtaking. But they weren't in the Arctic, she reminded herself, they were in the *desert*. And the stunning building in front of her wasn't fashioned out of ice, but out of the purest white marble.

The magical effect it conveyed was heightened by the setting sun, its rose-gold rays bathing the construction in an ethereal light.

On either side of them, as they drew nearer, she saw two spectacular marble fountains whose graceful jets seemed to reach up towards the heavens before plunging back down to earth again. The sound of rushing water was surprisingly soothing, and effortlessly created an oasis of contemplative calm.

She thought she would like to sit by them on her own one day, and reflect on the amazing chain of events that had brought her here. But for now, with her arm linked in the crook of Zafir's, she was content to let him guide her and Sami down the ornate mosaic-tiled walkway that led to the main entrance of the building.

She was still using a walking cane to lean on, but knew that soon, thankfully, she would need it less and less. Her ankle was indubitably healing. As for Sami—he walked alongside his father with his usual boyish spring in his step, agog at all the splendour around him and for the moment rendered speechless by it.

There were two uniformed guards standing to attention by a pair of tall, intricately decorated twin doors that stood beneath an impressive arched stone doorway. On seeing Zafir, they immediately bowed. Acknowledging them with a smile, he seemed genuinely pleased to see them, asking them both about their health and their families.

Seemingly satisfied with their response, he remarked that he was pleased that all was well with them. But when all was said and done he was still the King of the realm and he was soon indicating that he needed to move on.

He told Darcy that he was taking her to meet his mother…the woman their people still referred to as the Queen.

Although she was understandably nervous at meeting the Dowager Queen Soraya el-Kalil there was also a fair amount of excitement pulsating through her veins. What would she be like and would she really welcome a commoner as her new daughter-in-law?

Well, it was too late now because the deed was done. She and her son, the King, were already married.

They had to negotiate a large expanse of marble corridor before being led by a retainer to the private suite of rooms designated to the ruling Sheikh's mother. Straight away they were shown into the sitting room.

The first thing that surprised Darcy was how homely it was. Although there were some mouth-wateringly beautiful pieces of furniture, and sumptuous Arabian furnishings, they weren't overly ostentatious, and she was further reassured by the array of family photographs that resided on practically every surface. She itched to examine them more closely, certain that there must be some of Zafir as a boy.

But just then a woman who couldn't be anything *but* a queen gracefully appeared through an inner arched doorway and stopped all her thoughts in their tracks.

She was robed in ivory silk, and her hair was as black as a raven's wing with a stunning silver streak at the front, made more evident by a regal chignon. Her face was truly beautiful. She had winged dark brows and incredibly glossy ebony eyes and the smile she directed at them all was unstinting in its welcome.

Darcy owned to feeling relieved.

'My son… It is so good to see you!' Affectionately placing her hands against Zafir's cheeks, she stood on tiptoe and kissed him. 'I trust you had a good journey?'

'We did, indeed. Everything went according to plan, as I had hoped.'

'That is good. And now we get to the important part… You must introduce me to your wife, and also to my long-awaited grandson.'

'Mother…I'd like you to meet my wife, Darcy.'

'Oh, my goodness let me look at you, my dear.'

Her new mother-in-law carefully took her free hand in hers and held it. Darcy was surprised at the strength in her grip. She was not holding back on thoroughly examining the newest member of her family, but she never once lost her generous smile as she did so.

'Zafir has told me that you resemble a fairy princess, but I confess I thought that must be love talking. I see now that he was right. You are absolutely exquisite, my daughter.'

For a moment the younger woman didn't know what to say. The Dowager Queen really believed that Zafir *loved* her? How long before she realised that wasn't the case—that he'd only married her because he wanted to claim his son and heir?

'You are very kind, your Highness.'

'I only speak the truth. I also thank you for raising my grandson on your own until you reunited with his father. It must have been very hard to manage work and child-rearing under such circumstances?'

Flushing, Darcy responded. 'My mother was a great help to me, and I've always done the very best I could by Sami…after all, he's the light of my life.'

'Bless you for that, my child. Talking of which—it is time I met a certain young man.'

Sami was shuffling from foot to foot, as though his energy couldn't be contained. That told her he was excited. But he stilled when his new grand-mother approached. She greeted him with the same enthusiasm with which she'd greeted his father, only this time she leant down so that she was nearer his level.

'I am so pleased to meet you, little one. I am the mother of your father, the King. That makes me your grandmother.'

'I already have one of those. Her name is Patricia. What's *your* name?'

Soraya affectionately kissed the top of his head and said fondly, 'You may call me Nannaa. That is the usual name for my role in this country.'

'Cool…then I'll have a nanny and a *nannaa*. I hope I won't muddle them up.'

'I doubt that you will, my son. You are far too clever for that.'

Crouching down beside him, Zafir dropped his arm round the diminutive waist and gave him a squeeze. Darcy felt an inward glow of pride as she watched the pair. She was even more gratified when she sensed that Sami was happy with the new arrangements. He might even *welcome* them.

She made a mental note to talk to him about his feelings later.

Soraya had straightened, and her interested glance encompassed them all. 'Tell me, what do you want to do about eating? Are you ready for something now or would you like to rest a little before supper? If Sami is hungry—which I have no doubt he *is*—I will order some food to be brought here, and I can get to know him a little while the two of you go to your rooms and rest a while.'

Zafir's charismatic dark gaze turned immediately to his wife. 'Would you like to do that? It will give my mother the chance to talk to Sami on her own and you can have some private time to recover from the journey.'

'If that's what Sami wants…'

'I do, Mummy—and I'm very, *very* hungry!'

'That's settled, then.'

Darcy stole a fond kiss from her son before

they left him. Whilst she welcomed the prospect to rest and recover from the long journey, she couldn't deny the sense of elation she felt at knowing that she and Zafir would be spending some precious time alone.

The last time they had been intimate had been on their wedding night. After that they'd had to stay in London for a few days before they left, in order for him to finish some important work at the bank. He would be working late most nights and starting early, he'd told her.

Not being with him had been hard to bear. His closeness hadn't just become important to her, it was fast becoming *essential*. But for now she wouldn't let the thought scare her as it usually did. She would just have to learn to trust that he wanted this closeness as much as she did.

Zafir owned to a huge sense of relief. Things had gone better than he'd hoped. His mother had already fallen for her grandson, and she had embraced Darcy with admiring eyes and a full heart.

Now, all his senses tightened with anticipation as he showed his wife into his personal suite at the palace. It was spacious and cool at the same time, as well as undeniably grand. But as he closed the doors he frowned when he saw the thin sheen of sweat that had broken out on her brow.

'I think you need this rest more than you know,' he said, concerned. 'I am sorry if I presumed too soon that you were back to full health.'

In answer, her determined glance told him she was already garnering her strength *and* her defences. But her plump lower lip quivered and the action betrayed the vulnerability she fought so hard to hide.

'You haven't presumed anything. I really am stronger than I look and I recover quickly,' she insisted.

Zafir knew it was time to employ some tact. 'That may be so, but I still think you should go and lie down. It will give me a chance to unpack and change out of these clothes. I can find something more suitable for you to wear too.'

Placing his hand beneath her elbow, he gently steered her towards the bedroom.

'When you wake, we can discuss things some more.'

It didn't take long for Zafir to deduce that his wife had succumbed to a naturally deep sleep. Before she'd lain down on the canopied double bed she'd let him remove her shoes and had given him her jacket to hang up. He'd stolen a brief, necessarily restrained kiss from her lips then draped a light merino shawl over her. Her eyelids had closed straight away.

Whilst he couldn't deny he was disappointed that he couldn't join her, to express just how much he'd missed her these last few nights, he decided he would take the opportunity to ring his brother Xavier and ask him if they could meet up for their long overdue confidential chat.

CHAPTER TEN

DARCY SCREWED UP her eyes, then blinked to focus her attention. When she saw where she was—lying on a grand canopied bed the size of a small living room, no less—her heart sped like one of those intercity trains to King's Cross.

Where was her husband?

Did he think it rude of her to abandon him and their son so quickly? Had she already risked his good regard by behaving like this? They must both be as tired as she was after their long journey. The ebb and flow of emotional turmoil would surely drain *anyone*.

Then she remembered an incident that made her stomach lurch guiltily. Zafir had kissed her just before she'd fallen asleep. If she'd given him the slightest encouragement, shown him that she welcomed that brief brush of the lips, then he undoubtedly would have joined her and not been in such a hurry to disappear. But in truth an overwhelming weariness had seized her, as if all the events of the past few weeks had finally caught up with her, and she'd begged for respite.

Rousing herself, Darcy got to her feet. She turned on the embossed gold lamp beside her and light illuminated the now nearly darkened room.

Grateful to find that her husband had thoughtfully left out for her the flat open-toed sandals she'd packed, she silently thanked him. Tucking her feet into the cool leather shoes, she patted her hair, glanced briefly into a nearby mirror to check her appearance, then pinched her pale cheeks to restore some much needed colour. Finally she collected a shawl and her walking cane and limped across to the door.

The first thing she would do, she decided, was to go and check up on Sami. She prayed that by now he would be seeing the whole episode as one big adventure and not be too upset by events. And as soon as she was able she would send a message to her mum, to assure her of their safe arrival.

Stretching out her hand to fasten it round the brass door handle, she felt it open as if by magic. It was Zafir.

He was dressed in cool white cotton pants and a baggy shirt. He'd left his long hair loose and wore a beaded pendant round his neck and a couple of interesting bracelets on his wrists. One was fashioned out of some eye-catching gold coins and the other was made from twisted strands of softened black and copper leather.

In spite of not wearing his traditional robes, he still looked magnificent. As their gazes met and clung Darcy was glad of her walking cane to help steady her.

'You're a sight for sore eyes,' she teased him tentatively, unsurprised at the quiver in her voice.

'It's good to be able to dress casually from time to time. Where were you headed off to?'

Entering, he closed the door behind him. Without asking, he linked his arm in hers and led her back into the room. Immediately she sensed hot colour seeping into her face. It was becoming something of a trademark for her, she was sure.

'I wanted to check up on Sami. I didn't mean to fall asleep for so long. Has he had something to eat yet, do you know? He must be hungry. Goodness only knows what kind of mother you must think me...'

The expression on his face melted her to her core. His black eyes crinkled sexily and the dimples in his bronzed cheeks were out in force. Once again she regretted not inviting him to join her earlier.

'You are like the Madonna herself, my angel... pure, selfless and devoted to her son. I feel blessed to have found you again.'

'You definitely know how to melt a girl's heart, Your Highness!' She grinned, feeling more elated and sure of herself than she'd ever felt before.

'If all it takes is just a smile and telling you how important you are to me to elicit such a response, then I truly am blessed, Darcy.'

Carefully examining him, she lightly caught hold of his hand and enquired, 'So what have you been doing with yourself while I was sleeping?'

'I was making sure Sami was all right, of course, but it seems that my mother has already assigned herself his chief protector. She has fed and watered him and presently he is fast asleep in his new bedroom, with the Queen herself keeping a close eye on him should he need anything.'

Darcy frowned and again felt guilty. 'She doesn't have to do that. He's really asleep? He almost never does that so easily. I know he napped for a little while on the plane…it must be because he's out of his routine.'

Zafir nodded. 'He is probably much more accepting and relaxed about the situation than we realise. He's a four-year-old boy, remember, who has suddenly found himself in the equivalent of Wonderland.'

'You're right. I suppose I worry too much. But, that aside, what else were you doing after you left me asleep?'

Tucking a swathe of luxuriant hair behind his ear, he answered, 'I was arranging a meeting with my brother, Xavier, for tomorrow. We haven't met up for quite some time, I'm sorry to say.'

'Do you want to tell me why?'

'I think you can probably guess.'

'You mean because you weren't entirely convinced that we weren't having an affair? Do you now think you might have made a mistake and it's made you rethink your actions?'

Turning over her slim palm to examine it, he commented huskily, 'That and the fact that I met up with one of the bank's head secretaries, Jane Maddox, before we left—do you remember her?'

Darcy nodded. 'Of course I do. She never liked me from day one.'

'That's because she's a bitter, jealous woman— as I found out. She deliberately didn't tell me about your messages. No doubt she told her cohorts to do the same. If she could do that, then what's to stop her from lying about you having an affair with my brother? Anyway, I got rid of her. And when Xavier and I meet tomorrow I will know for sure.'

'You mean you sacked her?'

'That's the prerogative of being CEO.'

'So you'll ask Xavier again what really happened and find out if he lied to you after all?'

'Let us not worry about that right now. I have already made my pledge to you, Darcy, and that will not change. My son and I have been brought together at last and that means everything to me.'

'I see.'

'Don't look so sad. Everything will turn out well, I am sure. In the meantime, my mother wanted me to tell you how excited she is about the wedding and that—with your approval, of course—she will be organising it.'

'That's…that's very good of her. Do you know when it will be?'

He sighed. 'We're hoping for the beginning of next week. That will give me the opportunity to declare the day as a public holiday. Do you think your mother would like to fly out and join us? I know she was at the ceremony in London, and professed not to mind missing this one if she had to, but perhaps she was just being polite. I can easily arrange her travel, if you like?'

'I'm going to ring her soon. I can ask her about it then. What about what Sami and I are going to wear? Does *our* apparel have to be traditional?'

'As it will be a royal wedding—of course. Are you hungry?'

'What…?'

When he looked at her with that carnal hungry gaze of his, as if he could eat *her* for dinner, Darcy could barely think straight, let alone answer with an uncomplicated yes or no.

The handsome Sheikh moved in even closer and tenderly tipped up her chin. 'I asked if you were hungry. We will have to go in to supper shortly, and I need to know if you require anything in particular?'

Moistening her lips, she turned her startled blue eyes fully on his face. 'I'll have whatever everyone else is having. I don't have any preferences.'

That made him chuckle. 'My, my… When did you start to become so easy to please?'

She pouted. 'That doesn't make me a pushover, if that's what you think. I just want to make life easier for people.'

'What about making it easier for *you*? I have another question. Do you want to take a bath and freshen up before we go to eat?'

'That would be great—if I have time?'

'You can take as long as you like. I know that a lady doesn't appreciate being hurried.'

'Good. Then can you show me where my things are and I'll go and do just that.'

The Sheikh and his brother Xavier met at the official Offices of the Monarch in Zafir's private quarters.

In Zafir's opinion, his younger sibling seemed noticeably happier, and he was well dressed in a tailored suit with his dark hair grown a little longer than usual. Yet when he sat down in a colourful Rococo chair, with attractive motifs and intricate scrollwork, and Zafir indicated that he wanted to discuss certain significant events from the past, he grew distinctly uneasy.

'There is something in particular that I'd like to know. Did you lie to me that day about what you and Darcy were doing when I found you both in my office? Had you tried to force yourself on her? If you had, and did so to make me think you were having an affair, what on earth possessed you? Did you perhaps think I needed taking down a peg or two? Have you *any* idea of the torturous outcome of your cruel thoughtless behaviour?'

Flushing guiltily, his brother was immediately contrite. 'I didn't deliberately set out to make you suffer, Zafir...'

His opening words caused Zafir's stomach to plunge painfully.

'My actions were the consequences of my being greedy and immature. What happened has been a heavy burden on me for such a long time. I am very glad to have the chance to clear the air and set things straight.'

Shifting in his seat, Xavier wiped a hand across his perspiring youthful brow.

'Your secretary—Darcy—was the most beautiful woman I had ever seen. When she didn't respond to my attentions favourably, it wounded my ego. I took it as a personal insult. Who did she think she was, refusing the interest of the Sheikh of Zachariah's brother himself? Knowing that you'd made her your personal assistant, I was eaten up with jealousy and a red mist came over me. How *dared* she turn her back on me?

'Like the vain, insecure boy I was, I decided to pay her back by making it seem as though *she* was the one chasing *me*. I kept my eye on the door and arranged it so that you'd find the two of us in a compromising position. I gave her no opportunity to defend herself. So, yes, I *did* force myself on her. I didn't hurt her, but the thing is… I know my behaviour was despicable.

'Do you think I don't know that? I was truly

ashamed of what I had done when you fired her. I never wanted you or our family to think badly of me, but I was honestly glad when you eventually gave me my marching orders and sent me home. It gave me a much-needed opportunity to come to my senses.'

Taking a deep breath in, Xavier slowly released it.

'Can you ever find it in your heart to forgive me? I'm a different person now. I like to think a *better* one. I would never do such a thing again in a million years. You know that I am married now, with a beautiful little daughter. I am absolutely dedicated to my wife and family and I live in fear that something untoward might disrupt that happiness. I cannot put it more clearly. But my life is in your hands, my brother. Our mother tells me that you are getting married yourself, and that your fiancée is from England. May I know her name?'

Zafir didn't immediately answer. Xavier's

glossily dark hair flopped onto his brow and he impatiently pushed it back again.

Twisting his hands together in his lap, Zafir straightened his formidable shoulders. A spasm of sorrow flashed across his brooding dark gaze.

'I think you already know her name. It is Darcy...the girl I fired because of you.'

The younger man was visibly shocked. 'You are serious?'

Zafir's daunting black eyes stared back at him. 'I would not joke about such an important matter. I have a son by her. She was pregnant when I fired her—and, trust me...no one in the world could be as sorry as I am about that. Not just that she had my child, unsupported by me...that's bad enough. But because I acted so abominably.'

'May Allah forgive me... This is nothing less than a nightmare.'

Pushing restlessly to his feet, Zafir moved his head from side to side. 'It would be for me too, if I hadn't had the presence of mind to marry her in London, before we came home. Having the big heart that she has, Darcy decided not to keep me from my son and confessed all to me. But it still makes me ashamed that I made her suffer so needlessly and for so long.'

'I can hardly believe that you have a *son* by this woman!'

'His name is Sami.'

'And…and you've *married* her? Does that mean that you still have feelings for her?'

Impatience flashed in Zafir's eyes. 'What do *you* think, Xavier? Of *course* I have feelings for her. I— Never mind that. Darcy should be the one to hear first how I feel. I'd strongly advise you not to speak of this with anyone but me.'

The younger man also got to his feet, swallowing hard. His tone was gravely serious when he admitted, 'I have done you a great wrong, My King. If you banished me from the kingdom for the rest of my life I could not blame you. Your wife must truly despise me.'

'I do not think she has it in her to despise *anyone*. Her forgiveness seems to know no bounds—

even though it is probably to her detriment, I'm sad to say.'

'And… What about you? Can *you* ever forgive me for what I did?'

Expelling a long sigh, Zafir grimaced. 'I have thought about this for a long time. Following Darcy's example, I feel I should at least *try*. It is no excuse, but you were young—and very, very foolish. But, as my wife has also said, I want you to know that I am no pushover. If you attack me, verbally or otherwise, I will defend myself in whatever way I deem necessary. Call me a fool, but I am giving you one more chance to help make things right. From now on I want no more lies or deceit. If you transgress this edict *one inch*, be sure that I will cut you out of my life for good.'

Duly chastised, Xavier moved across to him and unhesitatingly hugged him hard. 'I am truly grateful for this chance. I will not disappoint you by word or deed again—I swear. From now on you will hear only praise from my lips.'

With a wry grin, Zafir set him apart a little then laid his hands firmly on his shoulders. 'I like to think I'm not so egotistical as to expect *praise* from those I love. But a little respect never goes amiss...'

Last night's lovemaking had left her tingling all over. Zafir had been so tender and thoughtful, but still breathtakingly passionate.

In the early light of what promised to be another flawless sunlit day, with her spirits raised and her heart filled with hope more than ever before, Darcy washed and dressed.

Zafir had already left for his meeting with his brother, and she eagerly went to find Sami and her mother-in-law. She tried not to think too much about what would transpire between the two brothers and determinedly hoped that things would go well.

The two women and Sami enjoyed a healthy, nutritional breakfast and chatted easily. The bond that was already forming between the young boy and the gracious matriarch was becoming more and more evident.

Around midday, when Zafir still hadn't returned, Darcy found herself restlessly walking through the beautiful palace gardens with her companions. Idly chatting about this and that, Sami and the Dowager Queen seemed almost to forget she was there.

As soon as she was able to, without seeming rude, she slipped away to sit on a charming bench in front of the cascading fountains. At first she fell into something of a dream. Then she mentally shook herself. All she really wanted to think about was her husband. It was as though her feelings for him knew no bounds.

Their heady lovemaking last night had left her feeling especially womanly and satisfied, and she wondered how soon it would be before they repeated the exercise. Doubt and apprehension had finally dispersed, leaving her with a real sense of well-being and happiness. Zafir hadn't yet told her that he loved her, but sometimes loving intentions could be just as powerful as words…such as when he had so gently and carefully helped her to bathe, treating her as though he wanted nothing more than to meet her every need…

Darcy was wearing the eye-catching yellow kaftan his mother had gifted her with, plus a gracious silk cowl edged with gold, to protect her pale skin from the sun, and when he at last found her Zafir thought she looked utterly adorable. His heart soared at the sight of her and he knew then that he wanted to make her feel the most treasured and happy woman on earth.

Any previous hesitation he might have had, fearing her feelings might not be as strong as his, had all but disappeared—like the foreboding black clouds that heralded an oncoming storm. Following his discussion with Xavier that morning, his brother's frank testimony had helped Zafir make his peace and remember everything that was good and meaningful in his life.

Stealing silently up behind his wife, where she

sat on the elegant white bench, he gently lifted the silken cowl that nestled against her shoulder and planted a tender kiss at the side of her neck. Breathing in her exquisite personal scent, he found himself longing to demonstrate his feelings more freely…

'Mmm…that was delicious.'

'You're back.'

Her mouth curved softly with pleasure and when he moved round in front of her Darcy was fiercely glad that he had come. It seemed that not a single moment went by without her feeling impatient with desire to have him close again.

As if attuned to her every need, he carefully sat down beside her. Falling easily into the richly dark gaze that reminded her of molasses, she played with his long hair and trailed her fingertips down his cheek.

'So…how did the meeting with Xavier go? Did he tell you the truth about what happened that day?'

Appearing more serious than usual, her husband nodded assent. 'Yes…he did. What can I say? I was appalled to learn I had been so gullible, so easily taken in. Whatever I may do for you and Sami in the future, it will never be enough to make up for my dangerously foolish behaviour. I let my love for my little brother make me blind to the truth, even though in my heart I suspected he might be lying. Can you forgive me for making you suffer so?'

'You didn't do it on purpose, Zafir.' She softly touched her palm to his bristled cheek. 'I don't think either of us expected our feelings to grow as strongly as they did, and maybe the power of those feelings blinded us to what was going on around us…'

'You unselfishly include yourself in that scenario when you have no need to.' Her husband frowned. 'Where did you learn such selflessness?'

Lifting her elegant shoulders in a shrug, Darcy mused, 'I suppose if I *have* learned such an attribute it must have come from my late father.'

'If I'd ever had the good fortune to meet the man, I know I would have admired him immensely.'

'And he you, Zafir. He wasn't impressed by wealth or position, but he knew a truly *good* man when he met one. What about your own father? You told me you cared for him very much?'

Sighing, he slid his hand over hers and held it fast. 'He was my rock and my mentor as well as my father and King. He lived his life by demonstrating strong values and a code of ethics that our people still try and adhere to. They didn't just admire him—they wanted to reflect those values in their own lives and show the rest of the world that it was possible to live in harmony.'

'And did he achieve that?'

His answering smile was gentle. 'I like to think he came close. There will always be wars and dissension the world over, but he didn't let that stop him from trying to be a peacemaker. I am far more argumentative, and I give way to anger much more easily than he did.'

'But I bet he saw qualities in you that he was immensely proud of and loved you nonetheless?'

Chuckling, Zafir leant forward and affectionately kissed her on the mouth. 'You must know by now that I've always been impressed by you, Darcy. Not just for your beauty and grace, but for who you *are*... From the moment I met you, when you became my assistant, throughout our affair, and even after I stupidly told you to go, I always knew I would never find another woman like you.'

'You shouldn't tell me things like that... It might give me a big head, thinking that I could turn the head of a *king*.'

'What? You mean the knowledge could possibly lead you to becoming *unbearable*?'

'Not a chance, Zafir. I only want you to feel that you've made the right choice in choosing me to be your wife. If I know that, then I'll be as docile and sweet as you could wish.'

'Never!' He laughed. 'If you became like that

then you wouldn't be the feisty and sexy woman I fell for.'

Her expression caught somewhere between hope and delight, she flung her slim arms round his neck and rained down avid kisses on his face.

'I'm glad that you like me just as I am and don't want me to change. In turn, I want *you* to know that I absolutely adore you and our son. If I can live with both of you for as long as for ever, then I'll think myself blessed beyond measure.'

'I echo that statement entirely, My Queen. Now, do you think we might slip back to our suite for a while? Sami is probably quite happy to spend some extra time with his grandmother, and we won't even be missed.'

'Did anyone ever tell you that you're a very *bad* influence?'

She squealed when he lifted her high into his arms for answer, and unhesitatingly carried her across to the mosaic walkway that led to his rooms.

On the way his guards caught sight of the couple, and whispered what she hoped was something complimentary, even envious, beneath their breath.

She smiled like a cat that had got the cream…

CHAPTER ELEVEN

'MUMMY, ARE YOU smiling because Daddy makes you happy?'

In the large stylish chamber where Zafir had allocated her a beautiful desk to write letters and answer correspondence, Darcy sighed contentedly and reached down to her small son to lift him onto her lap. He was a warm bundle of flesh, bone and sheer deliciousness, she thought affectionately as she pressed her lips to the back of his neck.

She loved him beyond distraction.

'Yes, your daddy makes me happy,' she told him, 'and so do you. I adore both of you, more than words can say. But there will always be a very special place in my heart just for you, Sami.'

The curly-headed little boy grinned, showing

his teeth. 'I like it when you talk to me like that… all lovey-dovey.'

Ruffling his hair, she laughed. 'You're just a great big softie.'

'What's a ring-bearer, Mum? That's what I'm going to be at the wedding, isn't it?'

The mention of the wedding was guaranteed to give Darcy the jitters. She could hardly believe that the big day had nearly dawned.

For the past few days preparations involving her wedding dress, correct royal etiquette, trying on the exquisite jewellery that was traditionally passed on to the Sheikh's bride, as well as perusing the guest list had consumed her. Whilst she didn't know most of the invitees, her mother-in-law had assured her that she'd invited not only the most prominent people, but many ordinary citizens as well and that there was nothing for her to worry about. She would be there to steer her right.

That was easy for *her* to say. The glamorous Dowager Queen came from a highly privileged world, whilst her new daughter-in-law *didn't*. But Darcy was determined to keep her feet firmly on the ground and take things in her stride.

As for Zafir—he had been just as preoccupied. Probably even more so. What with the preparations for the wedding, and visiting as many of the disadvantaged and sick as he was able to in the lead-up to making his official vows, he was also keeping himself apprised of what was going on with his businesses in London and New York.

When Darcy had asked if she could help, by going with him on his visits, he'd told her that it was traditional that the new bride shouldn't be seen by the public until the wedding. Frustrated, she was consoled by the fact that tomorrow night would be their official wedding night, and their guests could hardly complain if the bride and groom absented themselves early to go to their rooms.

'A ring-bearer is the person who carries the wedding rings for the bride and groom. We call them page boys in England, but I think that ring-bearer sounds magical. It's like a name out of one of those fantasy stories you so love. In any case, I think you'll look fabulous in your new clothes.'

'You *would* say that, Mum.'

'Your dad would say that too…and Nannaa Soraya and Nanny Patricia.'

Satisfied, if a little embarrassed by all the attention he was suddenly receiving, Sami jumped off his mother's lap and ran to the door. He called out, 'I'm going to play football with Rashid. I'll be in the big garden.'

Giving her son a reluctant wave, she called back, 'Well, be good…and also be *careful*. I don't want you hurting yourself before the wedding.'

'I will!' he yelled.

'Was it your idea or your mother's to have this little soirée before the wedding?'

Giving the exquisite blonde he'd already married back in London a knowingly indulgent smile, Sheikh Zafir el-Kalil of Zachariah found himself still warring with the possessive urge to steal her away and take her somewhere where they could be alone.

Gently steering her into a closeted corner of the vast communal living room that already teemed with people, he dropped his hand to her slender waist in the charming lapis lazuli dress she wore, noting that it perfectly highlighted the shade of her vivid blue eyes.

'It was my mother's idea and I didn't want to deny her. She's waited a long time for me to get married *and* to sire an heir. Celebrating her heart's desire is the least I could do, and in my opinion a small party won't hurt.'

'And you don't mind all the other things you have to do besides be the star attraction at the wedding?'

'I won't be that on my own. Everyone wants to see *you* too, Darcy.' The black eyes strayed meaningfully over her features. 'But I don't deny it's my role to be seen and ensure that my people are happy.'

She grimaced a little. 'That must be quite a

hard expectation to fulfil. I meant to make sure that everyone else's needs are met and yet still have time to enjoy the celebrations yourself?'

'My father taught me from a young age that my position was above all a privilege, and that first and foremost I should help to take care of our people not just by visiting those in difficulty when I could, but by demonstrating good values and morals. He told me that would be a big part of my remit as the country's royal heir, then their King.'

'You're looking very serious all of a sudden. Do you think you've been trying to do a bit too much?'

For answer, Zafir pulled Darcy into his arms, right then uncaring as to who might be looking at them, and reassured that no one would interrupt.

'It's a serious undertaking, being the country's Royal Head of State, but it definitely has its compensations.'

Helpless to do anything else but happily agree,

she tenderly laid her hand against his cheek. 'Oh...? And what are those?'

'Wait until we're alone in our rooms and I'll show you.'

It had been a long day and a tiring one, threaded through with a whole gamut of emotions and perhaps a bit too much champagne... God only knew how she would fare tomorrow, Darcy thought as a perfectly attired manservant suddenly appeared and handed Zafir a note.

They were standing together in one of the more intimate gardens, where all kinds of exotic aromas pervaded the air. As for their well-heeled guests—the majority of them had already left to make their journeys home.

Before she went to bed, Darcy decided, she would look in on Sami and give him a kiss, even though he was likely fast asleep. But right now the dazzlingly bright full moon was working its magic and it tempted her to stay a little longer and contemplate her extraordinary good fortune.

'Thank you, Amir. I will see to it.'

As he turned his attention back to his wife it was clear that Zafir was perturbed by the note's contents.

Tucking a loose coil of buttery gold hair behind her ear, Darcy frowned. 'Is it anything to be concerned about...the note, I mean?'

Smoothly depositing the missive into an inside pocket, Zafir patted down his silken robes. 'It's just an old friend—a business associate, really. He only wants to say a quick hello and wish me well. Go back to our rooms and I'll join you there.'

His matter-of-fact tone was obviously meant to reassure her. But, no longer as enchanted by the silvery orb that spectacularly lit up the inky dark sky, Darcy was disappointed that she couldn't wax lyrical about it with her husband.

Her spirits somewhat dampened, she automatically turned her cheek towards him to accept his kiss and answered, 'Okay. I'll see you later, then.'

Evidently reluctant to leave, he remarked, 'It

will be *sooner* rather than later, my angel. That's a promise.'

Yet her heart was filled with unease as she watched him walk away and very soon lost sight of him. His tall, broad-shouldered figure had quickly been swallowed up by the darkening shadows. Hugging her arms over her chest, she made herself stay a bit longer, to breathe in the scented air and contemplate what their future together might bring.

Since he'd received that note, she suddenly found she didn't feel so optimistic any more… He'd been worryingly reticent to talk to her about it.

Breaking into her reflections, the sound of a sultry female voice reached her. It might have come from anywhere. Beyond the flickering lanterns that had guided their way along with the brightness of the moon it was still dark. But it was what the woman was saying that rendered Darcy rigid as a statue.

'I *had* to see you alone, Zafir. I wanted to tell

you that I made the most terrible mistake when I agreed to let you go. Our relationship meant so much more to me than I let on. It was never just a convenient arrangement, as you thought. I've been in love with you all along, my darling.'

'*What?*'

'Yes, I'm in love with you…can't you tell? You know I would never have come here if I didn't think there was a chance you might feel the same way too. Can anything be done to bring this marriage of yours to a quick end, so that we can be together as our families always hoped we would?'

The man's reply was low and gruff. 'You stun me, Farrida. You say that you *love* me?'

Darcy had no desire to wait and hear any more. It was as though she were a fragile sheaf of corn being pummelled by the wind.

Still limping, she fled as fast as she was able, not knowing where she was heading. Her only certainty was that she had to get away. The urge to escape, to move as quickly as she could away from the scene and gather her wits, had never been so strong...

Breathless and tired, she finally stopped trying to run. Aside from the nagging ache in her ankle, it would be easy to get lost in the vast acreage of the gardens. Even in her haste to get away she'd had the sense to note a couple of helpful landmarks. But it was only when she dropped to the ground behind some high hedges to rest that the full impact of what she'd just heard sank in...

Had Zafir ever really cared for her at all? Had he fooled her into thinking he did just because he wanted to be close to his son? Did he plan to take him away from her?

Darcy didn't realise she was crying until the tears started to gather under her chin and trickle down onto her gown. If this was heartbreak then she knew it intimately. She knew despair too, but she wouldn't let either of them break her, she decided. She might not have the wealth and powerful connections of Farrida, and she had not been Zafir's childhood friend, but she wouldn't give up her child—no matter what they threatened or did. She would rise up and fight for what was right, despite it all.

Somehow, amidst the torrent of violent emotion that deluged her, a sense of calmness and purpose found its way into her blood. The impulse was stronger than she thought, and it quelled the urge to escape. It was hard to believe that she'd started to think clearly again, but she had.

Could a man *really* pretend to be so enamoured of her and treat her as if she was the brightest star in his galaxy if he was in love with someone else? It didn't seem feasible. No, whatever happened she would fight for her man—he was the love of her life and the father of her child.

Farrida might have decided at the eleventh hour that she loved Zafir, but one thing was for sure: Darcy loved him more…

Being summoned by Farrida to his private gardens in order to hear her tell him that she'd always loved him and then demand that he should bring his marriage with Darcy to an end so that they could be together was more than a bolt out of the blue—it was the epitome of the woman's arrogance!

All it had done was remind Zafir of how spoilt she was. She couldn't bear not to have anything she wanted handed to her on a plate just because she *wanted* it...

Zafir decided that he'd had a lucky escape.

Having put her in the picture and told her that meeting Darcy was the best thing that had ever happened to him, and that she was already his wife, he had almost felt sorry for the woman when she'd burst into tears, sobbing that he'd betrayed her, and then hurried off in search of her driver to take her home.

The unfortunate episode had made him even more anxious to return to wife. She'd wanted to share her charming reflections with him in the moonlight and he'd abandoned her to talk to Farrida. Now all he wanted to do was go to her and take her in his arms again...

When he returned to their rooms to find that Darcy wasn't there he was immediately concerned. His mother and Sami had long gone to bed, so he presumed she wasn't with them. Straight away he checked with some of his retainers and asked if they'd seen her. When they answered that they hadn't, Zafir really started to worry. At last, when one of the attendants clearing away after the party said that he'd seen her hurrying off down a path that forked into two separate gardens, his heart hammered hard.

What on earth was she playing at?

Not even pausing to take someone with him to help search, he headed off into the dim undergrowth, confident that he knew the grounds intimately enough to search alone.

But after a good hour had passed, with neither sight nor sound of her, he knew he should return and have the palace thoroughly searched. But first he would go back to their rooms and hope against hope that Darcy had somehow found her way back…

* * *

Relieved to have found her way out of the gardens, Darcy returned to their luxurious suite, undressed and donned a powder blue silk nightgown and robe. Then, in the dim lighting that discreetly lit the hallway, she carefully made her way to her son's bedroom.

Initially she'd given her mum the option of sharing her grandson's room when she'd arrived for the wedding, but the older woman had declined because Sami had told her that he wanted to be a big boy now and not a baby.

Zafir had allocated his mother-in-law a sumptuous suite down the hall, full of every luxury and feminine requirement she could wish for, and had stated that he was pleased to know his son wanted his own space—it meant that he was growing up.

The comment hadn't exactly reassured Darcy... She didn't want her little boy to grow up too soon.

Finding Sami asleep in a bed that was one size

up from a traditional single, she saw that he had kicked off the sumptuous counterpane and was sleeping on his front with his arms spread over the pillow. His hair was a tangle of curls and he might easily be mistaken for a girl. But she knew that when he sat up, the curls would fall naturally into place, and that the firm cleft in his chin and his already decisive jaw—so like his father's— would definitely declare him to be a boy.

Knowing her worries would feel eased if she was at his side she removed her robe and carefully sat down on the bed. Pulling back the covers, she snuggled up next to him. It was a comfort just to smell his scent and give him a cuddle.

In a few short seconds Darcy sensed her eyes start to drift closed. Another moment passed and sleep reached out to embrace her.

Just before she succumbed, a hauntingly handsome face floated into her mind. It was Zafir's.

'Why did you have to go to her?' She moaned softly. 'Aren't I enough for you?'

Remembering her resolve, she determinedly

pushed away the idea of his falling for the sultry Farrida's declaration of love and reminded herself of all the things *she* had that the other woman didn't…especially the beautiful son that their loving had made…

Zafir was shocked and distressed when he found that Darcy still hadn't returned to their rooms. Sweat was trickling freely down his neck under the heavy fall of his hair. Even the long loose tunic he wore beneath his robe felt oppressive.

'She should be in bed,' he said out loud, his heart hammering wildly beneath his ribs. 'Where *is* she?'

Adding to his irritation, he was still furious that his ex-fiancée had taken it upon herself to put in an appearance on the night before his wedding. He'd told her never to try and see him again—at least not in private—and that she categorically would not be welcome.

There was only *one* woman who mattered to him above all others and that was Darcy. He would shout out his feelings about her from the rooftops if he had to, and tell *everyone*…

As if a light had suddenly dawned, Zafir knew *exactly* where to find his wife.

Shrugging off his robes, he dressed in jeans and a tee shirt and headed down the corridor to his son's room. Before he entered he shoved his hands through his hair and briefly took stock of events. Then he gently opened the door.

Even at a distance he saw the golden sheen of Darcy's hair as it spilled down over her shoulder. He also saw Sami's abundant curls. It still gave him a thrill to know that this beautiful little boy was his, and would one day reign over this kingdom as his ancestors had proudly done before him.

Crossing the room to the bed, he bent over his wife to gently wake her. Her skin radiated warmth and softness even before he touched it, and it made him want to slip in beside her. But, knowing he wouldn't be satisfied with that alone, he whispered her name against her ear, then brushed his lips against her cheek.

'Darcy? Where did you get to? Let me take you back to our bed. I didn't mean to be away from you for so long.'

Her big blue eyes opened and stared. 'You're back? Don't worry about helping me to our bed. I'm happy to stay right where I am…really, I am.'

'But I'm *not*. I'm taking you back where you belong.'

Giving her little chance to refuse, Zafir reached towards her, peeled back the covers and lifted her out of the bed to hold her firmly against his chest. Then he stooped down to rearrange the covers more securely round Sami.

Murmuring, 'Let's go,' he turned and carried her out of the room.

Carefully kicking the door shut with the heel of his boot, he wordlessly transported his precious cargo to their bedroom. When they got there, unable to help himself, he let his hands linger as he carefully laid her down on the bed.

'Why didn't you wait for me here? I came back to find you gone. A member of my staff told me he saw you hurrying out to one of the gardens. What happened? Why did you run away?'

Sitting up, Darcy leant back against the plethora of plumped-up silk pillows and folded her arms. It didn't take a genius to work out that she was cross.

'I didn't wait for you in our rooms because I knew you were talking to your ex-fiancée.'

The colour drained from Zafir's face and his answering sigh was audible.

'You heard us? I didn't seek her out, if that's what you think. She showed up unannounced and said she wanted to talk to me. I didn't even know she was here until I received her note.'

Darcy sucked in her cheeks 'So what kind of *business* did you do together? That's what you said, wasn't it? That it was from a business associate? Or need I ask?'

Impatient and rattled, he dropped down beside her on the bed. 'We didn't do *any* business together. I broke off my engagement with her when we were in London. You *know* that. She clearly didn't take it well, and when she knew I was back in Zachariah she followed me here. Am I going to be punished by you for the rest of my life for having had a brief engagement to her?'

'She told you that she loved you.'

'You heard her say that?'

Darcy nodded. 'I did.'

'And did you hear me tell her that I was stunned by the confession? I never showed her by word or deed at any point that I reciprocated the feeling, and I certainly wasn't going to indulge her little fantasy and call off our wedding. The truth is that even if I didn't know already she has such an unattractive trait, this has only served to prove to me again how arrogant she is.'

'She sounded upset.'

'Forget about Farrida. It's you that means everything to me—you and *only* you. I went crazy when I thought you might have run away.'

The expression on his face truly mirrored his fear and despair, and it echoed Darcy's feelings when he'd told her to go…that he never wanted to see her again. He'd been torn then between loyalty to his brother and an unknown future with a woman who, although she was his lover, had not yet taught him that she would never lie to him.

It had been a testing time for them both. She certainly didn't want to hold any more blame in her heart towards him.

'Why would I run away from you, Zafir? My home is here, with you and Sami. I'd be a fool to run away from my heart's desire. Besides…I'm tired of running. No matter what transpires, I intend to be here for you, through the dark times as well as the good. Isn't that what we promised each other when we got married?'

Zafir was visibly moved by her heartfelt words. 'I hardly feel worthy of receiving such devotion… not when I've visited so much sorrow on you,' he confessed. 'I wish I could rewrite the past and make everything as it was when we first met. Life seemed so full of promise then. Yet now, having declared how you feel about me, you need never fear I will ever take it for granted. Knowing you has changed everything for me. It was only when we first made love that I realised my heart wasn't impenetrable after all.'

Without hesitation, Darcy gently wrapped her arms round his strongly corded neck and smiled into the ebony eyes that she loved beyond measuring. Tenderly, she asked, 'Are you saying that I broke down those impenetrable walls that very first time?'

'What do *you* think?'

'I think that love is like a miracle. And that no matter what happens it can't ever entertain the idea of punishment. But I've learned that it can and *does* involve forgiveness. We've both been hurt, but we've been given the chance to right the wrongs of the past. We shouldn't throw it away. Instead we should bravely face our future together and live the very best life we can. Don't you agree?'

'And you can really find it in your heart to forgive me?'

'Unreservedly I can—and *do*.'

Before he bent his head to kiss her Zafir honestly thought himself blessed amongst men to be given this second chance at happiness when he'd been so close to ruining everything. But his wife was a forgiving soul unlike any other, and when their lips met the blood in his veins throbbed like the most wondrous life-giving elixir, making him willing to live any number of lifetimes—rich or poor—if he could live them with her by his side as his wife and soul-mate…

CHAPTER TWELVE

THE DAY OF the wedding dawned especially fine and clear and the expectant buzz in the air was almost tangible. Her mother-in-law told her that all the omens were good ones, and Darcy smiled and hugged her. Throughout her dressing for the ceremony, in the silk and voile gown and delicately beautiful headdress that had been made for her, the excitement and pleasure she experienced was beyond anything remotely imaginable…

The folk around her seemed to feel the magic too. Smiles and good wishes abounded, and for the first time in her life she sensed that she could rest in the knowledge that she was honestly loved and admired. And it was all because of the incredibly handsome and generous-hearted Sheikh she had already married.

Even on this, their royal wedding day, Zafir was still accepting the kind wishes and prayers of those in the kingdom less fortunate than others, and the palace doors had been opened not just to the well-heeled guests who had travelled from afar but to the local population, who wanted to pay their respects and who undoubtedly thought themselves blessed under his rule.

When it came to the wedding itself the bride's vivid blue eyes moistened at the beauty of the ceremony, and at the reverent and uplifting sacred text that was spoken over them. When she looked at her groom—resplendent in his magnificent robes on a day that meant so much to both of them—and intoned the words that told the world she was unreservedly becoming his wife and helpmeet, she meant it with all her heart.

Then came the moment when Zafir declared that he would be her husband, father of her children, soul-mate and ever-present consolation, and she sucked in her breath when she saw that his silken ebony eyes were damp with tears.

At the closing instruction from the celebrant that he could now kiss his bride Darcy walked into his arms and met his kiss as though experiencing the touch of his lips for the very first time. As for her husband—he was in no hurry to shorten the gesture. He deliberately took his time, and the crowd around them gave a cheer that raised the rafters.

The feeling of his mouth against hers was more wondrous than ever, and she couldn't help but find herself excitedly speculating as to how many more children they would have together. They would be the children of a wonderful dynasty. And their darling little brother Sami had already cemented their parents' undying love for each other by helping to bring them back together when they had believed all was lost...

It was after midnight when they left to travel to the secret location that Zafir had arranged for their wedding night.

Darcy had been unbelievably fêted and spoiled, before *and* after the magnificent ceremony, and still the surprises showed no sign of relenting. But when they arrived at their destination, after travelling there on horseback—on a pure black stallion that Zafir owned, she in front and he behind, holding the reins—she was enchanted by the magical sight that met her eyes. The generously-sized Bedouin tent that nestled under the stars between palm trees and golden desert sands took her breath away.

'Am I dreaming?' she murmured as Zafir tenderly helped her down from the saddle, his dark eyes glinting like the most desired jewels in the kingdom.

'If you are, then I thank Allah I'm in the same dream.' He smiled.

The tent's interior brought even more enchantment. With its saffron-coloured satin walls, gold lanterns and beaded chandeliers, it was straight out of a fairytale. The scent of agar along with the alluring aroma of seductive herbs and spices hung in the air, and as Darcy breathed in the atmosphere her gaze strayed helplessly to the vast canopied bed in front of them. It was draped with gold damask and turquoise and arrayed with matching pillows, and never had a bed looked more inviting…

As Zafir moved to stand behind her, his big hands resting on her shoulders, she automatically leant back against his chest and sensed herself melt.

'Are we…? Should we?'

'Get into bed?' he finished, his voice smokier and more seductive than she'd ever heard it before. 'Of course.'

He carried her there, planting hot kisses on the side of her face and neck as he went. Even as she tried to kiss him back he dropped her unceremoniously onto the bed, peeled off his boots and lay down beside her. He was both heavy and strong, and she revelled in the realisation that he was about to make her his again.

The urgency she was feeling made her throw caution to the wind. But even as Darcy tore at his clothes Zafir matched her by stripping her of hers, and in a few short moments he had plunged inside her, filling her with his heat and silken hardness like never before, his bunched biceps helping to support him, his long hair brushing tantalisingly against her skin.

'Look at me...' he breathed, and there was a note of command in his voice as his mesmerising gaze hungrily possessed her.

His body and mind were in total tandem, leaving her in no doubt that he wanted her above all others—not just for now, but for ever...

It was then that he started to move inside her more slowly, urging her to wrap her legs round his torso, and the undeniable sense that he was taking her close to the edge before she tumbled headlong over the precipice gripped her wantonly.

When the moment of surrender finally came Darcy was hypnotised by the depth of feeling and emotion that deluged her. As her hips bucked against his her eyes were drowned in tears.

'I love you...' she breathed. 'I've *always* loved you.'

In answer, he kissed her hard, and his body

started to move more urgently. When he'd joined her at the other side of the precipice he dropped his head onto her chest until he could breathe more evenly again. When he could, he lifted himself up and smiled deeply into her eyes.

'I have always loved you too, My Queen. How could you even imagine I could love anyone else *but* you?'

'I've waited long enough for you to tell me!' she teased.

Zafir sighed and gently smoothed back her hair. 'My love for you has always been there in my eyes for you to see… But perhaps I should have been brave enough to tell you in words sooner rather than just show you how I felt?'

'You can tell me and show me as often as you like now that your secret is out.'

Darcy gave him a nudge and he accommodatingly rolled over onto his side. She quickly laid her arm over his chest and snuggled close.

'If I ever make the mistake of not telling you enough how much I love you I want you to remind me…frequently and *often*. Will you do that for me, my angel?'

'Yes, My King. That's the one thing I can honestly guarantee.'

EPILOGUE

One year later...

STILL DRESSED IN her simple white cotton nightgown, with the matching robe untied and her
golden hair freely spilling down over her shoulders, she went barefoot in a joyful skipping motion along the myriad marble corridors in search
of her husband.

He hadn't been back long from his business trip
to the States, and because he'd returned in the
early hours Darcy hadn't yet had the chance to
speak to him. Unbelievably she'd slept through
his arrival and, unselfishly, Zafir had let her sleep
on undisturbed. But as soon as she'd opened her
eyes she'd remembered that he was chairing an
important meeting in the opulent stateroom with
his board members early this morning, and de-

cided she wouldn't let any more time go by without seeing him.

To do so would be akin to being deprived of the capacity to breathe…

Meeting or no meeting—she would go to him and let him know in no uncertain terms just how much she had missed him.

A smartly dressed manservant in royal livery was guarding the double doors of the boardroom. When she told him that she wanted to speak to her husband the Sheikh, Darcy was surprised to be confronted by Rashid instead. The smile on his generous round face was warmly welcoming, as if Darcy were a trusted member of *his* family too, but she couldn't help but be disappointed that he wasn't Zafir.

Her bones *ached* to hold him. Two weeks was a long time to be apart from the man she loved.

'His Highness told me he wasn't to be disturbed, your Highness. It is an important meeting, but it should come to an end in about an hour.

Perhaps you would like to return to your rooms and dress before you meet with him?'

He lifted a kindly eyebrow at Darcy's semi-dressed state, in her nightgown and peignoir, as if he were a fond father who sought to remind her of the correct etiquette…

'I can arrange for a cup of tea and some crumpets to be made for you and have them taken out to the terrace, if you'd like?'

Disappointed at having her wishes diverted, the newest member of the royal family suddenly realised how inappropriate her clothing was. Reaching for the tie belt of her peignoir, Darcy pulled it tight and protectively folded her arms across her chest. Then she blew out an impatient breath and a long buttery ringlet drifted down onto her brow. She shoved it away.

'I know you mean well, Rashid, but food and drink is the *last* thing I can think about right now. If you knew how desperate I was to see my husband you would surely grant me a few short minutes with him…I promise I won't keep him much longer than that.'

Darcy detected the exact moment when the man's expression softened helplessly.

'You could persuade a rose to grow in the most barren part of the desert with a look like that, Your Highness,' he commented. 'Very well—I will see what I can do'

'Thank you. You're a treasure.'

Impatiently heading towards the closed doors of the stateroom, leaving behind his curious board members at the grand polished table, Zafir sensed his heartbeat accelerate uncomfortably. Rashid had told him that Her Highness needed to see him urgently, and that he presumed it must be important because she wasn't dressed yet.

Frowning, he immediately thought something must be wrong.

When he flung the doors wide and saw Darcy, pacing up and down, looking utterly adorable and sexy in a nightdress and peignoir that were almost sheer and that clung to her curves like the person-ification of temptation itself his heart raced even harder.

What was the woman trying to do to him? Surely she knew by now that two weeks without intimacy…hell, even *one night*—tested him to the very limits of his endurance? The only reason he hadn't immediately pulled her into his arms and made love to her last night, on his arrival back home, was that she'd looked so peaceful sleeping.

More importantly, she needed all the rest she could get right now, due to her condition. Zafir didn't want her to endanger the new baby…

When he spoke, his tone was more admonishing than he'd intended it to be. 'Darcy. What do you mean by parading in front of my retainers like that and putting them in an impossibly compromising position?'

'What are you talking about?'

Moving in closer and catching her firmly by the arms, he swept his simmering black eyes over her figure in a mixture of anger and frustration. 'Have you *no* sense of propriety, appearing like that in front of my men? Why didn't you think to dress properly first?'

'Why didn't I think to…to dress *properly* first?' she echoed.

Her teeth momentarily clamped down on her plump lower lip. In fact she looked as if she might even cry…

'I didn't think because I was in a hurry to see you. I didn't think about much else beyond that. Now I wish I'd been more—more *sensible*. God forbid if I've offended you.'

Wrenching one arm free from his grip, she looked as if she intended to get as far away from him as possible.

As if a rock had been dropped on his head from a great height Zafir flinched, then hauled her urgently into his arms.

'I merely wanted to bring it to your attention that you open yourself to all kinds of unhelpful speculation, appearing like that,' he breathed.

Somehow he found the smile that he'd wanted to greet her with.

'You're far too beautiful for any man to be confronted with first thing in the morning…and the last thing I want is for my servants to be lusting after you.'

The frown between Darcy's brows immediately disappeared, and he urged her even closer to his chest. Her scent was intoxicating…more intoxicating than honeysuckle-drenched air after a rainstorm. Zafir was already having trouble retaining his equilibrium.

'I want to kiss you. I want to kiss you properly and thoroughly. But I dare not do so right now. My board members will be alarmed if I don't return soon. Have you any idea just how much I've missed you?' He ran his hands gently down over her belly. 'You and the beautiful bump that will tell the world you're having my child.'

'*Second* child, don't you mean?'

'I've been wondering if this time it will be a girl…'

His remark clearly delighted her, and his wife dimpled. 'That's what I wanted to tell you. The doctor who'll be looking after me at the hospital rang to ask if I wanted to know the baby's sex.'

Zafir couldn't deny that he'd been delighted when his wife had agreed to have the baby born in Zachariah. It was the icing on the cake after all they'd been through.

He couldn't resist stealing a kiss from the side of her delectable mouth. Any more than that and he would be well and truly lost—certainly not fit to make any decisions at the board meeting.

'And what did you tell him?'

'I told him that it had to be a joint decision made with my husband.'

'I would not protest if you wanted to know.'

'I know that.'

Now it was her turn to steal a kiss. And as soon as her lips touched his Zafir groaned. His whole body irresistibly became more alive under her attentions.

'But would *you* like to find out…if it's a boy or a girl, I mean?'

Pausing to lift a swathe of coal-black hair from behind his nape, he smiled. 'My only preference is for the child to be healthy and for you to have a pregnancy that is as stress-free as possible.'

'Then I think it's probably best if we *don't* find out. We'll just have a lovely surprise when the baby is born.'

'I agree. Now, I want you to turn right around and return to our rooms. And if you decide to go back to bed and wait for my meeting to finish then I assure you that it will be finished sooner rather than later, my sweet.'

Another kiss was eagerly stolen. And, considering the circumstances, this time it lasted a little longer than perhaps was altogether wise…

* * * * *

If you enjoyed this story, take a look at these other great reads by Maggie Cox...
REQUIRED TO WEAR THE TYCOON'S RING
A TASTE OF SIN
Available now!

And why not explore these other
SECRET HEIRS OF BILLIONAIRES
themed stories?
THE DESERT KING'S SECRET HEIR
by Annie West
DEMETRIOU DEMANDS HIS CHILD
by Kate Hewitt
THE SECRET TO MARRYING MARCHESI
by Amanda Cinelli
Available now!